DEADLY WRONG

A Preternatural Affairs Novella

SM REINE

OTHER SERIES BY SM REINE
The Descent Series
The Ascension Series
Seasons of the Moon
The Cain Chronicles
Tarot Witches

The characters and events portrayed in this book are fictitious. Any similarity to real persons, living or dead, is coincidental and not intended by the author. All rights reserved.

http://authorsmreine.com/

Copyright © SM Reine 2014
Published by Red Iris Books
1180 Selmi Drive, Suite 102
Reno, NV 89512

Deadly Wrong

SM Reine

CHAPTER ONE

ISOBEL STONECROW NOTICED THE rot developing at the beginning of February.

Her fingernails' condition had become shameful in the last few weeks. It didn't seem to matter how much she washed her hands; the pig's blood she used in her rituals wouldn't come out from the edges and underneath the tips.

None of the grave dirt would wash off, either. Every little stain was a permanent mark on her skin.

It got worse quickly.

She was speaking with the spirit of a man named Vance Hartley when she accidentally ripped a fingernail off. She was beating on her newest bass drum with mallets, and she caught the jagged tip of her nail on the drum's beaded trim, and then it just came clean off. The entire thing.

Isobel finished the job anyway. She desperately needed the money—five hundred dollars—and she'd already spent the deposit, so she couldn't return it to the client.

The spirit of the dead spoke through her while

she was internally freaking out about the fact that losing her pinky nail didn't even hurt the way it should have.

With Isobel's help, Vance Hartley told his mother that he really had killed himself. That his death hadn't been foul play. That he had been horribly depressed for months, addicted to gambling, penniless, and without a scrap of pride remaining. It had seemed so much easier to hang himself rather than admit that he needed help to his family.

So he had killed himself. He'd just lost the suicide note down a crack in the floorboards, and he hadn't noticed until he was kicking at the end of the rope and couldn't go down to fish it out.

It wasn't the news Mrs. Hartley wanted to hear. She wrote a check for the remaining money and left the cemetery sobbing.

Normally, Isobel would have tried to offer a little extra help to Mrs. Hartley before she left. Crushed family members were outside of Isobel's job description as necrocognitive; once she had spoken to the deceased in question, her role in the family's affairs were over.

But most people did leave crying, so Isobel had printed off papers with phone numbers for resources. Suicide hotlines, grief-management therapists, that kind of thing.

That night, she let Mrs. Hartley go without speaking to her.

Isobel sat down on Vance's grave, legs straddling either side of the cross on the top, arms hugging the figure of Jesus, and inspected her pinky finger.

It was definitely gone. The skin underneath was black.

Still, she didn't feel any pain.

"Oh no," Isobel whispered, turning her hand to get a better look.

She hadn't been struggling to clean the pig's blood and grave dirt off of her skin after all. Her skin was actually turning those colors.

The flesh was rotting.

Isobel lifted her buckskin loincloth and checked the scratch on her hip. She had gotten that particular injury while arguing with one of the other death priestesses in Helltown. Isobel hadn't been paying attention to it; she'd always been a quick healer and assumed that wouldn't change.

The scratch hadn't changed in a week. It wasn't red or swollen. It wasn't scabbed, either. It was the same as the moment that she had scraped herself along one of the big wicker baskets they stored cadavers in.

She wasn't healing anymore.

Worse, she was *rotting*.

"I'm out of time," she told the indistinct figure of Jesus on Vance Hartley's grave.

He didn't offer any sympathetic words for her. Probably for the best—if a statue had started talking, Isobel would have started suspecting that her brain was rotting, too.

She *shouldn't* have been out of time, though. The only thing keeping her alive at the moment was her agreement with Ander, a demon crime lord who used magical contracts to bind people who were on the brink of death to his service. Like all his employees, she'd been "almost" dead when he'd picked her up, and the length of her service had a timer on it.

Isobel should have still had one month, two weeks, four days, and a few hours until her contract expired and she met the final death.

An entire month and a half to find a solution.

Yet her fingers were rotting, the cut on her hip wasn't healing, and Isobel was definitely running out of time.

It no longer seemed important that she was out of money to refuel her RV and feed herself.

Mrs. Hartley was the last client that she serviced.

It used to be that Isobel didn't have to worry about money at all. That had been a long time ago—literally another lifetime—but she remembered it in bits and pieces.

Before she had died and entered Ander's service, Isobel Stonecrow had been a lawyer. Her name had been Hope Emmeline Jimenez. She had come from modest beginnings in Manhattan, earned a lot of scholarships, and attended an Ivy League school. She had opened her own law firm and, by all accounts, done very well for herself.

She had also married a millionaire. Money really hadn't been an issue after that. Not for survival purposes, anyway.

But that had been another life.

Money was a problem now. It was the "now"

that mattered.

After Mrs. Hartley left, Isobel climbed onto the roof of her RV to watch the sunrise. Even though her panic was growing after losing her fingernail, Isobel didn't have many alternatives.

Her gas tank was running low. She'd have to cash that check in order to refill, which meant waiting for business hours. In the meantime, she couldn't reach any of her usual camping spots outside of Los Angeles.

So she rested on the RV's roof in the parking lot of a cemetery, waited for the sunrise, and lost herself in thought. The stars were dim, reduced to hazy blurs by the Los Angeles light pollution. Hard to tell how long she had until sunrise. She settled in for the long haul.

Isobel tried for the hundredth time to remember her wedding. She recalled some kind of gauzy white cloth. White heels. Ridiculously restrictive white underwear, corset and garters and all. She wasn't really sure that she had summoned those images from her memory or if they were just what she expected from someone like Hope Jimenez.

But she did remember meeting the groom at the altar. One brief moment where her veil was lifted, allowing her to see the man who she had agreed to marry. A handsome man, as angular and blond as Isobel was curvaceous and dark-haired.

Fritz Friederling. Demon hunter. Inheritor of his family's billions.

Her husband.

Isobel lifted a hand to look at her fingernails

again. It was dark enough that her hand was a silhouette without detail. But she could tell that she had nails on three fingers and a thumb, and then a twisted pinky with no nail at all.

Fritz would probably want to know that she was rotting.

It had been months since she'd spoken to Fritz or his aspis, Cèsar Hawke. If she didn't want to involve Fritz, then Cèsar might have been helpful for her not-so-little problem. He'd been a private investigator once; he had a penchant for brute-forcing his way through problems with a mixture of dumb luck and sheer enthusiasm.

Unfortunately, Isobel had hooked up with Cèsar before remembering that she used to be married to Fritz, and she had no idea what she was going to say to Cèsar about that. She didn't feel very sorry, but she also didn't want to continue her relationship with him, and he wouldn't take it particularly well.

He was a sensitive man, that Cèsar Hawke. And Isobel was allergic to awkward encounters.

It was stupid to avoid someone who might help because she didn't want to have to give him the "it's not you, it's me and my impending death" speech. Isobel knew that. But there were slightly less stupid reasons to avoid Cèsar, too.

He would have to use resources from the Office of Preternatural Affairs to help her. If the OPA caught on to the death witch who was dying from a bizarre, one-of-a-kind contract with a demon, she very well might have been added to the OPA's shelf of oddities.

Nobody wanted that, least of all Isobel. There really were fates worse than death.

Plus, Cèsar was incredibly loyal to Fritz. He'd definitely tell Fritz what was happening. And that spiraled right on back to the incredibly awkward conversations Isobel didn't want to have.

Isobel didn't need either of them anyway. She didn't need a *man* to save her, dammit. She didn't remember any of it, but she was an Ivy League graduate who had dominated dozens of difficult court cases, and she could save herself, thank you very much.

It was impossible to deny that she was getting desperate, though. Isobel had been searching for a way out of the contract for as many months as she'd been avoiding Cèsar and Fritz.

Honestly, she hadn't thought it could be that hard to circumvent death. She was a death witch and she knew practically every other death witch in America. They were a small community. One of them had to know a workaround, she'd thought. If not an actual way to end the contract, then a way to resurrect her as soon as it ended, or delay it.

But she was rotting, there was still no solution, and her husband would want to know.

She wasn't going to tell him.

Isobel just needed a little more time.

Unfortunately, all she had was one month, two weeks, and four days.

CHAPTER TWO

THE FIRST TIME THAT Hope Jimenez rejected a marriage proposal from Fritz Friederling, they had been on a yacht.

It had been the summer of 1998, and Hope seriously regretted the life choices that had led her to being on that stupid yacht. She wouldn't have even come to the party if someone hadn't needed to keep an eye on her roommate.

Hope didn't make it a habit to party in the weeks leading up to midterms. That was just asking for trouble.

But her roommate, Vena, had come from a conservative Mormon family and didn't know how to party safely. She was generously described as a "fucking moron" whenever she got into the liquor. *Someone* had to look out for her, even if there were tests coming up soon. Important tests.

The material was easy, but the tests were deliberately obscure. Entire books had been published about defeating those damn tests.

She should have been reading those books that night. Instead, she was at the open bar, watching

Vena get sloshed and dance with some other female law student. Hope wasn't sure if the rough ocean was making them flop around so terribly or if they were really that uncoordinated. Either way, it was embarrassing to watch. Hope hadn't stopped sympathy-cringing for hours.

Luckily for Vena, *everyone* was dancing terribly. She didn't stand out as particularly worse than anyone else, although there was something distinctly Mormon in the clumsy jerk of her hips and flap of her elbows.

At least they looked like they were having fun.

The bartender gave Hope another gin and tonic. It was only her second for the night. She was confident that the warm, buzzing disorientation in her skull had more to do with seasickness than the gin itself.

"You don't look like you're enjoying yourself," said the bartender. He was a narrow-shouldered man with black eyes and strangely pale skin. He looked like he belonged at a Black Death concert rather than working on a yacht.

"I'm enjoying myself," Hope said. "I'd be enjoying myself more if the boat would stop moving so much."

He smirked. "Maybe you need to lie down." Judging by his tone, he didn't mean for her to lie down and sleep.

She rolled her eyes and turned her back on him to enjoy her gin.

Vena and Tracy had draped themselves over some blond asshole now. Hope didn't recognize him—he wasn't in her class. She would have remembered his angular good looks, his slicked-back hair, the way he helped himself to handfuls of the girls hanging on to his shoulders. *Gross.*

This guy looked like exactly the kind of stupidity that Hope needed to protect Vena from.

She didn't have to venture onto the dance floor to rescue her friend. The slimeball strolled toward the bar with his new arm accessories. "Drinks for the ladies," he told the bartender. "Anything they want."

Hope peeled Vena off of him. Her roommate was so sloshed that she didn't even fight back. "I think they want glasses of water."

The blond man looked surprised to see Hope, as though he hadn't noticed her by the bar.

Once he spotted her, the familiar once-over followed. The slow look from her feet to her face, and then back down again to make sure that he'd seen that everything in between was really that good.

She hadn't dressed up for the party, but Hope was always meticulous in her appearance, and she wasn't shy about accentuating her natural assets. Specifically, the big ol' assets attached to her ribcage.

Seeing which parts of her body men examined first was a pretty reliable asshole test. Blond Guy lingered on her tits and never made it back to her face.

He'd definitely failed the asshole test.

Blond Guy carefully dislodged Tracy, propped her against a bar stool, and gave Hope his full attention. "I don't remember seeing you here earlier."

"Try again," Hope said.

"Excuse me?"

"That doesn't even pass for a pickup line. If you're going to hit on me, please come up with something cheesier so Vena and I can laugh about it once she's sober."

Amusement sparked in his eyes. "Would a marriage proposal work for you?"

"That's pretty bad, yeah. Who are you?"

"Who am I...?" Now the amusement had turned to a grin. "A better question is, who are *you*?"

"Hope Jimenez." She thrust a hand toward him. "Guardian angel of ladies too drunk to consent to sexual activity. The emotional equivalent of a designated driver."

"A hero." He shook her hand. His fingers lingered on hers. "And a witch."

She jerked her hand back. "Excuse me?"

How could he have possibly known about that?

Hope looked down at herself, expecting to see that she had grave dirt on her dress. She'd visited the cemetery before leaving for the party with Vena. But her outfit was clean. Her nails were clean. There was no sign that she had been hanging out with dead people, so there was no way this guy could know who—and what—Hope was, aside from a law student.

"You radiate," Blond Guy said helpfully, noting her confusion.

"That's getting closer to the shitty pickup line I was looking for." But Hope had lost some of her confidence. She smoothed down her bobbed haircut and checked her reflection in the mirror behind the bartender.

Meanwhile, Vena blew chunks all over the bar.

Hope grabbed her friend, pulling her hair back. It was too late. Vena's modest Mormon shirt was slick with vomit. "Damn! I need a bathroom." Her roommate chose that moment to slump into unconsciousness. Hope almost dropped her. "Ugh, and I need a bed, too. Are there any beds on this stupid boat?"

"Six," Blond Guy said. "There are cabins upstairs."

"What kind of assholes can afford a yacht with six bedrooms?" Hope muttered as she hauled Vena away from the dance floor.

Blond Guy stooped to pull Vena's arm over his shoulders, taking most of the weight from Hope. "This is the *Friederling X*, I think," he said. "So there are at least nine other Friederling yachts. They must do well for themselves."

Hope snorted. "Good for them." *Assholes*.

They deposited Vena in an empty cabin. Hope took her roommate's overshirt and shoes off and hung them in the bathroom. Blond Guy watched from the doorway with obvious amusement.

There was some vomit on Hope's dress, too. She scrubbed it off using towels that were monogrammed "FF" on the corner.

"You're not getting lucky with her tonight," Hope said, glaring at Blond Guy. Her suspiciousness hadn't faded at how helpful he was. "She's unconscious. Can't consent. Don't even think about it."

"I don't want to. I like my women awake and responsive."

"The fact you feel like you have to specify that is creepy." She rolled Vena onto her side so that she wouldn't choke if she barfed in her sleep. "You still haven't told me who you are, by the way." Hope tried to brush past him to leave the room, but his arm barred her exit.

"I'm your future husband. We're going to get married someday." He stroked his fingers over the back of her hand. "I think the ring will be your graduation present when you leave law school."

Everything about that statement was ridiculously insulting. Hope wasn't sure if she should laugh at him or slap him.

She decided to slap him.

He didn't move an inch, didn't even flinch.

But he lifted a hand to his cheek as if surprised that she'd reacted with anything but swooning agreement. "You really don't know who I am, don't you?"

"You're an asshole. Don't talk to me."

Someone started screaming.

The instant change in the attitude of Hope's would-be suitor was astounding. He went rigid and alert.

There was also suddenly a knife in his right hand.

Horror swept over Hope. She leaped away from him. "Don't hurt me!"

He let her go—didn't even try to attack. He raced down the hallway in the opposite direction.

Blond Guy kicked down one of the other cabin doors and jumped inside.

Hope's immediate instinct was to run upstairs to call the police. But that was a stupid urge, she knew. They were in international waters at that point. The cops couldn't do anything.

She was trapped on a yacht with a stabby creep and people were screaming.

"I should have stayed home to study," she told nobody in particular.

Hope edged past the open door that Blond Guy had kicked in. When she saw what was happening in the cabin, she stopped.

Vena's partner in terrible dancing, Tracy, was sprawled across the bed.

And Tracy was being eaten.

Not in the good way.

The pale-skinned bartender was crouched over her with his fingers buried in her chest. There was no incision, no wound; he had simply thrust his fingers into the bone knuckle-deep.

His head was thrown back in ecstasy as he devoured her in the way that only demons could. Because that was what he must have been: a demon. Probably an incubus, judging by the raging erection dribbling ichor onto Tracy's chest.

Hope's dad had warned her about all the common demon breeds a death witch might be unlucky enough to stumble across, including incubi. She hadn't encountered them before, but he wasn't hard to identify.

While Tracy was quickly spiraling toward death, Blond Guy was fighting with another pair of incubi. He moved so fast that she could barely track him.

Glass shattered, knuckles pounded against bone, blood sprayed.

Kopis. That was what he had to be—and it explained why he'd recognized Hope as a witch. Kopides were demon hunters. Men who were born with a natural propensity for slaughtering evil. They had been part of her early education, just like incubi and nightmares and mara.

Somehow, Hope had ended up on a yacht with a goddamn demon hunter and incubi.

The kopis in question looked much too busy to save Tracy. Hope's eyes fell on the lamp beside the bed. It was bolted down, like everything else on the yacht. It couldn't work as much of a weapon.

There was a power cord on the back, though.

Hope swallowed down her fear, edging into the room silently. The incubi that was attacking Tracy was still wrapped up in his little world of dreams, dragging her through hell and back again, just for fun. He didn't notice that she was approaching him.

She always carried a pocketknife on her. It was a useful tool to have—a little two-inch blade sharp enough to open packages, cut through zip ties, that kind of thing.

That night, it would be a murder weapon.

She sliced the cord open near the base of the lamp, fraying the wiring. It sparked at the touch of metal. Hope made sure to keep her fingers on the wooden part of the knife.

Then she jammed the cord into the bared knee

of the incubus eating Tracy.

Electricity leaped between the cable and his flesh. The lights in the cabin dimmed.

His eyes flew open, lips parting with silent shock. Sparks danced between his teeth. The shadow of his skeleton flashed through his pale skin as he jerked his hands out of Tracy's chest and fell backwards.

The lamp cord was too short to chase him with it. Hope tossed it aside so it wouldn't accidentally electrocute anyone else.

"What the fuck?" the bartender growled. He was recovering fast. Too bad—the voltage hadn't been high enough to cause real damage.

Electricity was one of the only things that could really hurt demons like him, or so Hope's family had told her. But she brandished her tiny blade anyway. Her heart was pounding with the terror of facing a demon—an actual demon.

"Conscious consent, asshole," Hope said. Her voice only quavered a little. "Is it *that* hard?"

"It is for demons," said Blond Guy, who was holding another incubus's head in one hand, fingers tangled in his hair. He had decapitated the thing.

The bartender took one look at his dead friends and bolted out the door.

Blond Guy followed. So did Hope.

"What's going on here?" she asked Blond Guy, skidding into the hallway a few inches behind him.

"This group of incubi has been contracting themselves out as wait staff for parties and killing people once they fall asleep," the kopis said. He was breathless but calm. Decapitating incubi was no big deal for him, apparently. "I lured them here so I could kill them first."

They chased the bartender outside. Hope reached the deck in time to see the incubus hurl himself over the railing and into the ocean. Either he was a great swimmer, or drowning was a slightly better alternative to dealing with the kopis on the yacht.

"You lured them here? What did you say your name is?" Hope asked when she finally remembered how to speak.

He gave her the faintest smirk as he approached the railing, stripping off his jacket and shirt, exposing an admittedly impressive set of abdominal muscles. "Fritz."

"Fritz what?"

"Friederling," he said, and he jumped over the railing into the ocean.

Isobel woke up in a graveyard. Not on a yacht. She was curled up on her side in the grass with dew clinging to her skin and a tombstone topped by a crucified Jesus a few feet away.

"You can't sleep here."

A female officer stood over Isobel—a pleasantly round-faced woman who looked more sympathetic than annoyed. Probably because Isobel had remembered to change into normal street clothes before falling asleep. The police didn't react quite as kindly to a half-naked woman in animal skins.

Isobel sat up, rubbed the sleep out of her eyes.

She immediately checked her pinky finger. It was still rotting. That hadn't been a nightmare.

"Are you okay? Do you need a ride to a shelter?" the officer asked gently.

"No, that's all right. Thank you." Isobel stood and dusted herself off.

"It's not safe to spend your nights somewhere like this."

"I fell asleep grieving." Not a lie. Isobel was grieving herself, the body she was losing, the contract she never should have signed. "I won't do it again."

The officer followed her to the gates. She watched until Isobel got into her RV and drove away.

Isobel only went to the next city park before stopping again. She still needed to cash Mrs. Hartley's check at the bank and probably shouldn't walk into civilization covered in the soil of Vance Hartley's grave.

She showered as carefully as she could, trying to wash off the dirt without also washing off any other parts of her body. As Isobel bathed, she drifted back on her newfound memory of meeting Fritz on the *Friederling X* yacht.

That had been the first time that Isobel had rejected Fritz's marriage proposal. It was a fun memory. Definitely one of the better things she was recalling from Hope Jimenez's life now that the magic of Ander's contract was starting to fade.

The second rejection had been four years after she died—after she lost all her memories of Hope Jimenez and became Isobel Stonecrow.

Isobel had moved to California when initially fleeing Ander. She'd picked the location solely because it was as far as she could get from him without sneaking into another country. The fact that Fritz had been working in Los Angeles was only a minor complication. She'd been afraid of him at first, worried that the kopis who had shattered Ander's business would expect repayment, but he hadn't bothered her for a long time. She'd had plenty of time to establish her own business and build a life in Los Angeles.

When he finally asked for repayment, it had been with the completely reasonable request to speak with his dead grandfather.

Easy job. Easy money.

Somehow, easy quickly turned into complicated, and then two months of dating. If anyone could call "holing up in Fritz's mansion to have lots of sex" dating.

It was brief and intense. The definition of a whirlwind romance. Fritz said all the right things, knew exactly what kind of clothes she liked and what size to buy them in, took her to restaurants that unexpectedly became her favorite, plied her with expensive presents.

Everything he did was right. He was charming as hell.

But it had all gone so damn *fast*.

The marriage proposal had surprised her at the time, and not in a good way. Dating an intense billionaire demon hunter was too overwhelming.

So Isobel had ditched him. Agreed to keep working with him if he needed it, but no more sex, no more presents, definitely no diamond rings.

He hadn't even seemed heartbroken at the time.

But Fritz didn't go away, either.

Now she understood why, many months later. Once she dipped into her memories with the help of Dayna, a priestess of the Hand of Death, Isobel had seen a wedding from her previous life. She'd been wearing a gauzy white dress and lifted her veil to see Fritz on the other side.

Isobel had thought that Fritz was just the kopis who saved her from Ander. Instead, it turned out that Fritz was Hope Jimenez's husband—and he was still waiting for his wife to come back to him.

Lost in thought as she showered, Isobel scrubbed her hip a little too hard. It was habit—her skin got scaly if she wasn't thorough with the loofah.

But now it peeled the cut on her hip wide. There was no blood. The skin ripped open an inch and exposed a little bit of decay underneath, where it had been developing unseen. The skin was greenish-purple.

She got out of the shower. Pulled on a bathrobe. Sat on her couch and tried not to cry.

One month, two weeks, less than four days.

Fritz wasn't going to have to wait for his wife in vain much longer.

CHAPTER THREE

ISOBEL ALWAYS FOUND FUEL for her RV one way or another. She hated resorting to theft, but she only had five hundred dollars from Mrs. Hartley; she had to be realistic about how much it was going to cost to survive for the next month and a half.

With a tank as big as hers, she had to siphon from multiple vehicles at the shopping mall. She went after the big ones. The SUVs, the Jeeps, the minivans. Isobel took a few gallons here and there, filling red gas canisters and carting them back to her RV before anyone caught her.

Her hip and pinky finger were itching.

When the needle on her gauge was over three quarters, she bought herself a bun from Cinnabon and headed north on the freeway.

Okay, she actually bought a dozen buns from Cinnabon. But she was dying. Life was definitely too short not to stuff her face.

Who was going to notice a few extra pounds on the zombie anyway?

Her RV hated going at freeway speeds, so she

kept it slow and ignored the people who honked angrily as they zoomed past her. She got better mileage when she went slowly anyway, and she needed to make it several hundred miles to Reno, Nevada.

That was where Isobel had left behind a young necromancer named Ann. She'd already been in contact with Ann twice. In fact, Ann had been the first call that Isobel had made when she learned that her contract with Ander had a looming deadline, since Ann could raise zombies as easily as Isobel rolled out of bed in the morning.

If anyone could resurrect Isobel, it would be Ann.

The problem was that Ann had already said she couldn't do it and wasn't interested in wasting any time to help Isobel. The young necromancer had valid reasons, which she'd shared bluntly with Isobel over a terse phone call.

First of all, trying to resurrect someone—not reanimate them, but resurrect them—was a huge energy drain that would require a human sacrifice. Sacrifice would draw unwanted attention to Ann. Second of all, considering the terms of Isobel's contract, she really needed a magical lawyer more than a necromancer.

Ann had said that part half-jokingly. "Magical lawyer."

In all seriousness, that sounded like a great idea to Isobel.

But no such thing existed. Ann was as good as it got.

Isobel had to convince her to try.

It was a nine-hour drive to Reno from Los Angeles without any major delays. Less than a day. Her RV had a pretty big tank of gas; if she were careful, she would only need to refill once to reach her destination. She could even probably top it off with a little bit of cash.

She barely made it two hours outside of the city.

The highway leading northwest cut directly through the desert. It was the fastest route, but unfortunately, less-trafficked than the other routes that she could have taken.

That meant there weren't any rest stops nearby when her RV began to splutter.

"No," she whispered, hands tightening on the wheel. "No, no, no…"

The vehicle bucked hard enough that the frame shivered, making her beaded curtains clatter. Glass bottles jangled in her cabinets. The engine moaned —actually *moaned*.

Isobel didn't know much about the mechanical side of things where her RV was concerned, but she didn't think that moaning was a good sign.

The gas pedal stopped working.

There was nothing in sight but empty desert.

Pulling the wheel to the side, her tires jittered as the RV moved onto the shoulder. She shivered to a stop a car's length off of the highway. About two seconds later, all of the lights in her vehicle died.

"Ugh," Isobel groaned, dropping her head so that her eyebrows bumped against the steering wheel.

This is not a promising start to one of the last days of the rest of my life.

The blazing sun beat down hot on her shoulders as she dropped to the dusty ground outside. There was no wind. Nothing but a hundred degrees of stale, miserable heat. It felt like she was going to catch fire within seconds of exposure. Hopefully that wouldn't be the case—Isobel was feeling awfully dry, and she had no idea how her zombiefied body would handle heat.

She popped the hood and propped it up with the metal bar inside. Something inside was smoking, but she couldn't tell what. She waved the air clear.

"Come on, baby, give me some kind of hint," Isobel muttered.

All the mechanical pieces lurking inside her RV *looked* fine. She twisted a few knobs, poked at the cables. There weren't any obvious leaks. Not that she would have known what to do with them even if there had been any.

How the hell was she going to get to Reno with this thing now?

Isobel's hands were throbbing. She flipped her palms over to discover that she had burned her fingertips while prodding at the RV. The skin on her left hand had melted away, leaving three of her fingers smooth and shiny.

It hadn't hurt. She hadn't felt that at all.

She sank to a crouch, back leaning against the RV, and dropped her face into her hands.

Isobel felt like crying, but even though her shoulders started to shake and her eyes burned, nothing came out.

The magic of Ander's contract was fading

faster.

Isobel wasn't sure how long she sat there, watching the sun move, trying to cry without leaking a single tear. She got up a couple of times to try to turn the RV on again, praying that it would have magically healed itself the way that she wasn't.

The shadows grew longer, a few cars passed, nobody stopped to help.

When she finally rounded the RV to start walking, maybe stick a thumb out to hitch a ride, the sun was nearly touching the horizon.

And someone was waiting for her.

There was a black car parked down the hill. It could have been there all day, for all she knew—she hadn't walked far enough in that direction to see it, and she hadn't heard it stopping behind her. The windows were tinted dark enough that she couldn't see who was inside, but she didn't need to see.

It was no surprise that Fritz Friederling would show up once she became desperate.

Knowing him, he'd had her followed for months anyway. He had probably been watching her every move. Waiting for her to get desperate.

His timing was perfect.

She tried to wipe her cheeks dry, even though there were no tears on them. It hurt to walk away from the RV, knowing that she might never get back to it. The thing might have been an antiquated piece of shit, but it was her antiquated piece of shit, and it had been home for years.

Isobel felt heavy as she approached the black

car.

The window rolled down. Despite the tinted windows, Fritz was wearing sunglasses. She could see herself in the reflection.

"Are you ready?" he asked.

Isobel clenched her hands into fists. Her remaining fingernails buried into her palms. "Ready for what?"

Fritz lifted an eyebrow.

Yeah, he didn't need to elaborate. He was asking if she was ready to give in to the magnetic pull of what his money could do for her.

She tried to ignore the squirming sense of defeat in her gut.

"Okay," she said.

The driver opened the door for her. Isobel slipped into the seat opposite Fritz, sinking into leather so plush that it consumed her body. The limousine was actually one of his cars that was more function than form; the minibar, television, and recessed lighting were meant to make guests comfortable, rather than anything Fritz enjoyed having in his vehicles.

He was a man who appreciated the grip of rubber on pavement. He liked nice damn cars for the sake of performance and the way they reacted to his touch.

The niceties of a limousine weren't interesting to him.

The fact that Isobel was starting to remember so much about Fritz's preferences bothered her.

"What will it be?" Isobel asked. "Have you hired the best covens to meet us at your private island to cure me?"

"I'd do it if I thought it would help. The only remaining possible solution is much more boring, though."

The limousine glided onto the pavement. Isobel couldn't even hear the engine.

She studied Fritz's features. His careful concealment of his thoughts behind the sunglasses had never worked on her. He was feeling just as frustrated and exhausted as Isobel.

She wasn't the only one grieving her impending death.

Isobel sagged, covering her eyes with her hands, trying to slow the growing ache in her skull. "I don't mean to sound ungrateful. I'm not angry with you. I'm angry at circumstance. I'm angry that I haven't been able to fix this myself. I'm a death witch—this shouldn't be so difficult."

Fritz slipped the glasses down the bridge of his nose. The whites of his eyes were bloodshot. "I know."

"I wanted to be able to save myself."

"Yes, I know."

His calm acceptance only made her feel more frustrated. "And the fact that you know so much about my reactions is terrifying. I don't like that you know me better than I know you."

"That will change when we fix the contract," Fritz said.

"I think Ann can help. The necromancer that we hooked up with a free ride to college in Reno. That's where I was heading."

But it wasn't where the car was heading. They

weren't going back to Los Angeles, either.

The driver had taken a side road off of the highway, leading them deeper into the miserable nothingness of the desert. She could just make out the glimmer of buildings on the horizon. A small town, maybe.

"Ann won't help you," Fritz said. "She's a necromancer. By the time your contract expires, it'll be too late for you."

"What do you mean?"

"When someone dies, their soul evaporates within hours. It returns to some kind of central pool of energy to be remixed, recycled, reborn. Not exactly direct reincarnation, but—"

"I know," Isobel said. "I *am* a death witch."

"You're already halfway there, Belle," Fritz said. "Halfway between here and gone. Maybe more than half."

She looked at her increasingly mangled hands again. Missing fingernail, blackening skin, burned fingertips. "So this is it," Isobel said. "Once the contract expires, I'm dead and gone."

"Not necessarily."

The buildings on the horizon grew. It wasn't a town after all.

It was an airport.

"There are some things money can't buy," Isobel said.

"See, now that's just not true," Fritz said. "That's something that poor people tell themselves when they're feeling insecure about their money. You *can* buy anything. You just have to know where and how."

The attitude rankled, even though Isobel was starting to think that was an attitude she had once shared with him. "Some things can't be fixed. At all. Cèsar killed Ander, and Ander was the only guy who could rewrite my contract."

"But there are demons far more powerful than he was," Fritz said.

The limousine paused outside the airstrip so that the driver could punch an access code into the gate. It was a relatively tiny airport. There were more helicopters than planes. Some of the hangars stood open. She recognized private jets inside a couple of them.

"We're going home, aren't we?" she asked, swallowing hard around the lump in her throat.

"Yes," Fritz said, sliding the sunglasses back over his eyes again. "We're going home."

Back to New York.

CHAPTER FOUR

IN THE BATHROOM OF Fritz's private jet, Isobel realized that she had scuffed her knees while fretting over the RV. It was a minor injury, so minor that she wouldn't have ordinarily given it any thought, but now her throat thickened with tears at the sight of it.

The scuffs made the skin over her kneecaps a little paler, a little rougher. Just some dry skin embedded with dust.

It was never going to heal.

She felt like an automaton returning to her seat for takeoff, stiffly buckling herself into the chair and accepting a water bottle from the stewardess.

Fritz was in the opposite chair. He spoke to her, but she didn't respond.

The jet took off.

Isobel wondered if she had been on it before. She didn't think so—it looked more recent than the jets she would have taken with Fritz. Maybe a new purchase with the Friederling fortune. She couldn't remember…yet.

The more broken Isobel's body became, the

more quickly complete memories returned.

It was because of the magic, she thought. Ander's contract was releasing its hold on her. The thick ropes of energy that had allowed her body to function as though she were still alive had also been holding the memories at bay, like a cloak over her mind.

As one thing slipped, so did everything else.

She felt it slipping faster now as fatigue set in. It might have helped that getting onto Fritz's private jet was far more Hope Jimenez territory than Isobel Stonecrow territory, too. The leather seats and eager stewardess triggered something deep inside her brain.

The sound of the jet engines lulled Isobel to sleep. Her head drooped against the side of her chair.

And she dreamed.

She dreamed of white sand beaches, turquoise water, and a cool, salty breeze. She dreamed of walking barefoot among the driftwood in a long white dress, holding a bouquet of tropical flowers that a florist had given her when she told him that she was getting married that day.

"Do you, Fritz Jeremy Friederling, take Hope Jimenez as your wife?" asked the officiant. He was a dark-skinned man with dreadlocks and a hint of a patois. He smelled pleasantly of sunscreen and sandalwood.

Fritz stood on the officiant's other side. He took Hope's hand. His fingers were wrapped around something hard and cold.

A knife.

There was mischief in his eyes as he passed it to her.

"I do," he said.

Hope felt the corner of her mouth lifting in a smile of her own.

Shrieks echoed over the beach as a crowd rushed toward them. The clamor had initially sounded like part of the slap of ocean against beach, but now it was distinctly an approaching horde.

They were running out of time.

The officiant spoke faster. "Do you, Hope Emmeline Jimenez, take Fritz Friederling as your husband?"

There was little room for doubt at that point. They were eloping thousands of miles from their nearest friends, family, and business associates. They'd spent weeks on the *Friederling X* together, sailing the warm waters of the Caribbean as Fritz hunted demons that threatened his international holdings.

And Hope, fresh out of law school, was enjoying every single moment of it. Even the bloody parts. Fritz always took care of her.

She never wanted it to end.

"I do," she said.

Fritz kissed her before the officiant said that he should. It was brief, a brush of lips against lips.

Then he whirled and plunged the knife into a demon before it could tackle him.

The fight lasted for over an hour, most of which Hope spent trying to stay out of the horde's reach. The officiant was a friend of Fritz's—a local kopis who had been trying to deal with the demon infestation for weeks—and he fought as fiercely as though he were a demon himself.

Between the two men, they were more than capable of holding back even a hundred fiends. They carpeted the beach in blood and bodies.

Hope's dress didn't even get stained.

It was everything that Hope had been trying to avoid by attending a nice, normal law school so that she could get a nice, normal job, but Fritz was pretty good at making that all seem okay. He was very convincing.

The officiant survived, somehow. So did they.

No demon walked off the beach that day.

Hope and Fritz spent the night in a penthouse overlooking the beach where they had gotten married. He had been injured and refused to let her treat the wounds. They got all kinds of bodily fluids all over that very expensive penthouse—blood and other things—and they left a generous tip before getting back on the *Friederling X*.

Happy times, both warm and bloody.

In the private jet, the intercom chimed. The pilot spoke. They were almost at their destination, and the sound of his voice woke Isobel up with a start. She felt raw, as though she had been crying. Her cheeks were dry, though. She didn't have tears anymore.

Fritz was still sitting across from her, working on his BlackBerry. "Sleep well?" He didn't even look up from his phone. There was none of that youthful liveliness in him, that mischievous spark that had made his wild proposals so impossible to refuse.

Isobel imagined that was just what happened to a man after he lost his wife.

"Fine," she said. "I slept fine."

Isobel was exhausted, but she didn't let herself sleep again, even when they got caught in traffic between the airport and their destination.

She didn't want to remember anything else.

Unfortunately, as they traveled through the dense streets of Manhattan, she started seeing a lot of things that stirred memories. Not just of her time as Hope Jimenez before she died, but of her time after signing the contract with Ander, too.

Isobel had sworn she would never return to New York. She'd planned to abandon more than one life there. "What's the plan?" she asked, forcing herself to look away from the buildings passing outside the limousine's windows.

"It took you long enough to ask," he said.

"I'm not feeling very talkative." She kept her tone measured, even though she considered using Fritz's necktie to slap him in the face a few times.

"I have a portal to Hell in my condo. We're going to go to the City of Dis and make an appeal with the Judge at the Palace to nullify the terms of your contract. We should be able to restore you to the condition that you were in before you signed."

He was so matter-of-fact about it.

Fritz had a portal to Hell and they were going to use it.

"Why the heck do you have a portal to Hell?"

Isobel asked. She knew that Fritz had some business dealings with demons; he'd never exactly been secretive about it. But she'd always assumed that they came to him.

"I have multiple pathways, actually," Fritz said. "Just the one leading to Dis, though. What do you know about the city?"

"I know that Ander worked there a lot." She left that dangling as an unspoken accusation.

"Most demons of any repute do work in Dis. It's the political and industrial center of Hell." Almost as an afterthought, he added, "Ander's former property isn't in that dimension, though. It was in one of the smaller worlds."

Isobel knew. She remembered. There had been no name for the wasteland that he'd lived in, and no occupants aside from Ander himself—she had discovered that firsthand, in the most unpleasant way possible.

Ander's front door had opened wherever he wanted it to open. While Isobel had been working for him, that had usually been somewhere in New York, or occasionally overseas. Every other exit opened into his Hell dimension.

During her one and only attempt to escape through a window, Isobel had ended up wandering the empty desert outside Ander's house. She'd only survived because it was nighttime. The shadows had permanently burned her flesh. If she'd escaped during the day…well, she wouldn't have a problem with her contract expiring, that was for certain.

"So you think this Judge can reverse the contract," Isobel said, shaking off the memories she wished she could have forgotten.

Fritz nodded. "Judge Abraxas has supreme authority over any deals other demons make, so long as they're members of the Palace court—which Ander was up until his death."

"How do you know I won't just die when this Abraxas guy releases me?" Isobel asked.

"You weren't dead when Ander took you. You don't have any mortal wounds right now, so you should be restored to good health." The way that he said "should" didn't inspire much confidence.

She studied the hands spread across her lap. The pinky finger with no nail in particular.

It sounded like a long shot, what Fritz was talking about. But it was also the only shot she had now.

"Okay," she said. "So we're going to Hell." No big deal, just a burning pit filled with demons. Couldn't be much worse than Helltown in Los Angeles. Or New Jersey, for that matter.

The limousine pulled into a parking garage underneath a high rise. Fritz took Isobel to the elevator and swiped a card. The number for the highest floor of the building illuminated.

It felt like it took hours to reach the penthouse, though it couldn't have been longer than a minute or two. They were greeted by a small lobby at the top of the building. It had marble floors and big windows with a view of the city that had probably cost eight figures.

Fritz had to swipe the key again to open the platinum-handled doors at the end of the hallway.

Two layers of security to reach the penthouse.

Very fancy.

"You live here?" Isobel asked.

Fritz stood back to let her enter first. "We both did."

She didn't want to enter the double doors now. Didn't want to see what was waiting for her on the other side.

"The portal's in the office," Fritz added.

She knew without having to ask that the office was on the second floor loft in the rear. There was no way to reach it except to go inside.

Gathering her strength, Isobel stepped forward.

The entryway of the condo was simultaneously strange but familiar. Without having to look, she knew that she would find leather couches to the right and could imagine the view she would see through the floor-to-ceiling windows to her left.

None of it suited her tastes. Everything was glass and steel. Pretty Scandinavian-looking.

Knowing Fritz, he had probably hired designers from Denmark to custom build all his furniture. Why not? With access to the Friederling fortune, the sky was the limit.

That thought came to her with a twist of disgust. She'd never been disgusted by Fritz's money before. Something else she was remembering from her life as Hope?

"You didn't always live here." Fritz shut the door silently behind them. "We had our own apartments in addition to this one. Yours was sold after your death, so I can't take you there, but it was less than a block from your law offices. Very convenient."

"Convenient," she echoed. As if it was normal to have a shared living space as well as independent living spaces.

She wondered if her private apartment had been as uncomfortable as the condo that she shared with her husband.

Even if her finances hadn't been limited, Isobel wouldn't have chosen to live anywhere but her RV. *That* was her style. Not necessarily the eclectic interior decorations—most of which were hand-me-downs from witchy friends—but the freedom of it all, the ability to pick up and leave whenever she wanted to, untethered to location.

Isobel couldn't imagine a life where she would have enjoyed this kind of condo.

Fritz was showing her around the kitchen now. He was rattling off the types of flooring and cabinets and how they had picked everything out to be the very best, but Isobel only had an eye for the two big ovens.

"Now this looks like something I'd enjoy," she said, opening one to peer inside. They were each industrial-sized, like something that she might have found in a restaurant kitchen.

He lifted an eyebrow. "Really?"

"Think of all the cookies I could make." Isobel was still feeling a little queasy from all the Cinnabon she had snarfed after her RV broke down in the desert, but baking still sounded *very* appealing.

"Where in the world did you pick up a baking habit?" Fritz asked with a weak laugh.

The fact that it surprised him left a weird

aftertaste on Isobel's tongue.

Who had she been if she wasn't the kind of woman who baked cookies for fun and lived in a billionaire's Danish dream house? Did she know Hope Jimenez at all?

"Some friends taught me to bake," Isobel said. "There's not a lot for humans to do in Helltown at night when you're on lockdown against nightmares. A couple of the other priestesses liked to make desserts. I only got good at cookies. Everything else was too difficult."

"Interesting," Fritz said in a way that made it clear he didn't find it interesting at all.

He didn't like to be reminded that she had changed any more than she did.

Isobel headed up the glass staircase to the loft, no longer waiting for Fritz to give her the grand tour. Their bookshelves didn't have a lot of books on them. Mostly, they were decorated with expensive crystal baubles, knives held aloft on stands for display, and a few globes that didn't depict Earth.

"Where's your private apartment?" She picked up one of the globes. It was semi-transparent, but heavier than it looked. All of the geographic labels were printed on the inside.

Fritz waved a dismissive hand. "I have a few."

"Any in Hell?"

"Yes. I have a place in the City of Dis."

"Have I ever been there?" Isobel asked.

"No. You weren't involved in any of my infernal dealings."

"Did I know about them at all?"

"Some." He was starting to look irritated. "You were busy with your own life, Belle."

She didn't like it when he called her Belle anymore. It had been kind of cute at first, since most of the witchy friends she picked up around Helltown called her the same thing, but now it grated. "What did we do together, then?"

Fritz's gaze went distant. "Plenty of things. Trust me. If we'd had more time, I think we could have conquered the world together."

The fact that he might have meant that literally was more than slightly disturbing.

"But after I...died...you ended up getting a government job. Why?"

"I didn't really want the world, Belle," Fritz said. "Once you were gone, I had to find something else to do with myself."

It sounded like there was a lot of missing story there. A very painful story that she didn't have the emotional stamina to hear.

She returned the globe to the shelf.

"I want to go to Hell," Isobel said. It sounded like the slightly more pleasant alternative to exploring Hope Jimenez's former life.

Fritz's mouth twisted. "Okay. Let's go to Hell."

CHAPTER FIVE

THE GATEWAY INTO HELL looked fairly innocuous, all things considered. It was a ring of stones around a burned patch of ground. Orange soil dusted the surrounding floor. The air smelled faintly of sulfur. It reminded Isobel of a poorly contained indoor fire pit, in a way.

Thick cables led from a hole in the wall to the circle of stones, ruining the fire pit illusion. Matching cables connected to the workstation in Fritz's office. Isobel took that to mean that the portal was somehow computer-controlled.

Pretty impressive for arcane infernal technology.

The room had been hidden behind another set of bookshelves in Fritz's office and didn't look familiar to Isobel, so she imagined that it was meant to be a secret room—and one that she had never been in before.

As if the creepiness of a hidden room wasn't good enough, the walls were also lined with steel and iron several inches thick, sort of like the door to a bank vault. Fritz left it standing wide open, so she had a great view of the layered metal.

"Not worried about anything coming through, are you?" Isobel asked, trailing a finger down the metal inside the door. It was as thick as her hand. The bolts that secured it while locked were two inches wide. It looked like it could have contained a nuclear blast.

"This portal connects directly to the only legitimate entrance into Dis, which is inside the Palace," Fritz said, grabbing a tote bag from the desk. "If anything comes through, it would mean the whole city has fallen. So no, I'm generally not worried about that." He handed the bag to Isobel. "Stranger things have happened, though. Demons aren't exactly predictable. Here, you'll want to dress yourself appropriately for the trip."

Isobel reached in to find a mass of leather. Her stomach curdled as she picked the pieces apart. He had given her leather pants, a leather jacket, even leather boots.

"This looks like something the nightmares in Helltown wear."

"It's armor," he said. "Hell isn't like Earth. The air's not friendly to humans."

"So where's your armor?"

"The Palace is heavily warded. I don't think I'll need protection. You, on the other hand, won't heal any injuries you incur for the time being. We should be careful."

So he had noticed. Isobel self-consciously curled her damaged fingers in the leather to hide them. "In that case, thanks."

Isobel stripped off her shorts and t-shirt where

she stood, leaving only her underwear. Fritz watched her closely. He wasn't looking at the more interesting parts of her body that Cèsar was charmingly bad at trying not to stare at, but at her hip and knees. The places where she was damaged.

"There's something else you need to know about the City of Dis," Fritz said. "Time runs at a different speed between dimensions. A day passing in Dis is a week on Earth."

Isobel wiggled her hips into the leather pants. They were a little too tight. He'd probably bought them in Hope Jimenez's size, and she had eaten far fewer cookies and probably went jogging or whatever else lawyers did for fun.

"How's that work?" she asked, sucking in her stomach to pull the pants up to her waist. "Time going at different speeds."

"Hell. Who knows?" He shrugged as though that should have been adequate explanation. "Your contract's tethered to the date on Earth, though. Probably why Ander never took you to Dis for work with him. He wouldn't want your contract to run out too quickly."

Isobel quickly did the mental calculations.

She had a month and a half left on her contract. About six weeks.

"So we'll have less than a week to fix this once we reach Hell," she said. "Uh, how long is it going to take for this Judge Abraxas guy to reverse things?"

"That's part of the issue," Fritz said. "We still have to get an audience with him. I'm pretty confident that we'll be able to—"

An alarm shrieked through the condominium, cutting him off.

A knife appeared in Fritz's hand. "Take this," he said, pushing it into Isobel's grasp before darting out into the office again. The reminder of their wedding day was so overwhelming that she couldn't breathe for a moment.

Isobel hurried to finish dressing, stuffing her generous breasts into a leather jacket that zipped from hips to throat before following him.

She found Fritz on the loft, sneering down at the entrance to their condo. "How did *you* get in here?" He wasn't speaking to Isobel.

"I used the door. What do you think you're doing?" The response was silken, the accent Italian.

Isobel peered around his elbow.

A tall, slender woman with her hair cut into a severe blonde bob stood in the doorway, flanked by a pair of guards. They were probably Union, judging by the fact that they wore the standard Bluetooth headsets and all-black clothing. Those guys were allergic to color.

"I thought I removed every Union camera," Fritz said.

"You did. You didn't remove all the motion sensors." The woman strolled toward them on stilettos. The fact that she could walk at all in such a snugly cut pantsuit was impressive.

"Isn't a man allowed to visit his private residence without scrutiny from the Office of Preternatural Affairs?"

"Not when I suspect he's been hiding a portal to Hell in his office." The woman mounted the stairs, giving him a smug, tight-lipped smile that gave Isobel the wild urge to slap her.

Isobel was surprised to recognize their visitor now.

"Lucrezia de Angelis." The name came to her easily, though it felt like something that she should have spit off of her tongue.

The recognition was, apparently, mutual.

Lucrezia's eyes narrowed. She almost missed a step climbing to the loft, and that clumsy little slip evoked a sick satisfaction in Isobel. "Hope? Is that you?"

"God fucking dammit," Fritz muttered. Louder, he said, "No, Lucrezia. This couldn't be Hope. You know that Hope died—"

"Almost five years ago, yes. I remember."

The bitch probably had it marked on her calendar.

Isobel had never liked her very much, and the feeling was mutual. Though she couldn't remember why.

Giving Fritz a sideways look, Isobel thought that she could probably guess where the animosity came from. Fritz's ability to pick up women hadn't been limited to the *Friederling X*. She was fairly certain that any attractive woman who came within fifty miles of him would have less-than-favorable things to say about the youngest son of the Friederling family.

Memory dawned. Just a flash of it. A naked, gyrating flash. "You cheated on me with her," Isobel said. "Oh my God. You *asshole*."

Fritz rolled his eyes to the sky, seeming to offer

a silent prayer to whichever deity had intervened to help return Isobel's memory to her rotting brain. "What a convenient time to get that information back."

"She isn't Hope, hmm?" Lucrezia asked.

Fritz held up a hand to silence her, focusing on Isobel instead. "The situation is more complicated than you recall, Belle. I'm going to ask you to withhold judgment until everything else is restored. Can you do that for me? Can we shelve this conversation for later?"

Isobel frowned at him. Memory was emerging, pressing hard enough inside of her skull that it felt like it might extrude through her forehead. It ached. With that ache came images.

Walking into their bedroom at the manor. Finding Lucrezia on top of Fritz, his body buried deep inside of hers, those surgery-perfect tits bouncing.

Isobel hadn't been angry. At least, she didn't remember any anger at discovering that. "I can wait," Isobel said slowly. She didn't really have a choice. She had no way to make sense of her emotions, these pictures she was seeing.

Fritz let out a sigh. "Good."

"Why are you trying to take your dead wife to Hell, Director Friederling?" Lucrezia asked. The question of how his dead wife had come to be walking around again didn't seem to bother her all that much. Considering that she was vice president of the Office of Preternatural Affairs, Isobel imagined that random dead people coming back to life probably wasn't very shocking anymore.

"We're taking a second honeymoon," Fritz said. "How did you get here so quickly? We've only just arrived."

"Your stewardess works for me. She informed me of your itinerary. You're not allowed to go to Hell."

He grabbed Isobel's wrist and pulled her into the office. Lucrezia followed them. "I'd love to debate interdimensional travel regulations, but I'm busy," Fritz said. "Mind getting out of my condo?" He reached for the keyboard on his desk.

Lucrezia stepped in his way. She stood too close to them, close enough that Isobel was almost gagging on her flowery perfume. "I'll have more than your job for this." Lucrezia's eyes glowed with triumph.

"Come on, Lucrezia. We'll be back before you know it. Don't make this difficult."

"Making your life difficult is one of my favorite things, Fritz," Lucrezia said.

"At least you're honest about it," Isobel muttered.

That got the vice president's attention. She glowered at Isobel. "Hope Jimenez. The fact that you're alive is probably another violation of OPA law. What did Fritz do to bring you back, hmm? Deal with the Devil?"

"Something like that," Fritz said, leaning in close to Lucrezia. He brushed a hand down her arm, sliding his hand around to cup the small of her back. His voice dropped to a murmur. "Wouldn't you like to know?"

The blonde woman swayed toward him despite

herself, as though she just couldn't resist.

He took a quick step forward, hit a button on the keyboard behind Lucrezia, and yanked Isobel into the portal room.

"Guards!" Lucrezia shouted.

The Union men rushed into the office as Fritz and Isobel rushed out. The portal flamed to life, flooding the entire room with a brilliant crimson glow. Fritz stepped up onto the stones ringing the edge.

"Come on, Belle!" he shouted over the roar of wind that blasted through the portal.

Isobel balked at the edge.

If she passed through, she was cutting her time even shorter. Six weeks to six days. She hadn't had time to consider whether she would rather risk that the Judge's decision wouldn't be in her favor or enjoy what little time she had left.

What would that do to the magic of the contract that was already fraying? Was she going to fall apart? Or worse—would she remember everything?

Fritz took the decision away from her. He jerked on her arm, hauling her over the edge of the portal.

The room swirled around them.

In the doorway, Lucrezia's mouth opened in silent protest, hand lifting to point at the gateway. The Union guards moved behind her.

Muzzles flashed with gunfire.

Nothing struck.

Isobel tasted the difference between worlds before she could see the difference. The stale air of the room was bitter on her tongue, faintly sulfurous.

It was a familiar taste that she had tried hard to forget. Unfortunately, Ander's contract had only wiped her memory of the time before she died, not the time that she had worked for him.

She would never forget what Hell tasted like. Not until the day she finally, permanently died.

Which was now less than a week away.

CHAPTER SIX

ISOBEL COULD ACTUALLY FEEL time accelerate as her body fell into Hell's slipstream.

She felt it in the way that the skin on her pinky finger flaked and peeled away. She felt it in the scabs on her knees, the way her nose and mouth and eyes dried out, and how the cut on her hip ached as it tore further.

Worse than any of that, she felt the magic releasing its grip on her mind, allowing Hope Jimenez to swell from the depths of amnesic oblivion.

Isobel spiraled, tumbling out of consciousness into memory.

It didn't come as a single coherent thread, as it had earlier. It came all at once in a swarm of images.

She was at her second wedding to Fritz—not the elopement, but the event that had been widely publicized among their families, friends, and business contacts.

Isobel was wearing a filmy white dress in front of hundreds of people at a venue that had cost six figures to rent. The only demons in attendance had been invited, and Fritz did not bring a knife to kill them.

"You told me you weren't going to expose my family to this," Hope had hissed to him over the phone, locked in a bridal suite with a team of professional stylists and her maid of honor. Calling Fritz was the only way they could talk. They weren't allowed to see each other on their wedding day, though they'd already been married for weeks. Her dad had insisted on the tradition.

"They're allies." Fritz sounded impatient with the conversation. He was probably being prodded by as many attendants as she was.

"They're *demons*."

"Demons can be allies."

"That doesn't mean that I want them at our wedding. My grandmother is here!" Hope had felt horribly panicked by the idea of demons at the ceremony. Specifically, the kind of demons that the Friederlings might have invited to his wedding.

She was afraid that someone might recognize her.

Why was I afraid someone might recognize me?

"Relax, Emmeline," Fritz had said, and he hung up on her.

Another hard tug of memory, and the memories pushed ahead to their official honeymoon, which had been as stuffy and over-planned as their official wedding. Because it had been a destination wedding, the honeymoon had been an extension of the festivities that included all the guests. Fritz had spent most of the time networking.

Networking with demons from Hell.

Nobody seemed to recognize Hope, and her family had gone home right after the ceremony, unable to afford the lengthy honeymoon festivities. Her family was safe. That was the important part. But she still hadn't been able to relax, and she found herself taking comfort in the open bar.

Even gin and tonics weren't enough for her nerves.

While Fritz was distracted, Hope had run into Ander. The very demon who had eventually saved her life but enslaved her in the process.

Isobel was surprised to remember meeting him so soon. She'd assumed that she must have met him through other channels later on. But no, it was definitely Ander at the Italian winery where they'd held their honeymoon festivities. He'd looked just as old and fat and miserable in a suit as he always had.

"You don't look happy." That was how Ander said hello, bellying up to the wine-tasting bar and taking the stool beside her. He'd been wearing contacts that hid his slitted, catlike eyes. Hope wasn't the only one praying to evade notice from Fritz's business contacts.

Hope put on a professional mask for Ander. She pretended to smile while watching her new husband chat with his grandparents, knowing that he would later turn around and use that same charm to make contacts with the owners of infernal businesses.

She wasn't the only one with a mask. Fritz was as two-faced as Hope, in his own way.

"I'm only tired from all the celebrations." She kept an eye on Fritz and her voice down. He was close, maybe close enough that he'd be able to hear their conversation.

But Isobel didn't remember the details of that conversation. She couldn't remember if Ander had already been trying to talk her into a contract, or who had invited him to the wedding.

She did remember that he was charming, but Ander had always been incredibly charming. He was fairly unassuming, a little bit grandfatherly, very effusive with praise. And he'd been particularly on top of his game at their wedding.

The fact that he vanished before Fritz returned to Hope's side didn't escape her notice.

Just like the way that Fritz was flirting with one of the bridesmaids before dinner didn't escape Hope's notice, either.

The magic of the contract continued to unravel, releasing floods of memory, trapping her deep in unconsciousness.

Isobel was whisked through Hope's life. Days and weeks blurred.

Shortly after returning from the honeymoon, Hope started practicing law.

She had refused to let Fritz finance the firm, though he had made a half-hearted offer more than once. She recruited the talent who worked in her office herself, used money that she had gathered from investors with minimal contribution from their "family" funds, began attempting to acquire clients via aggressive networking.

Hope worked herself to exhaustion. She was as

dedicated a lawyer as she had been a law student.

And her business was a complete failure.

No clients. No money.

Nothing worthy of her time.

"The work will come," Fritz said one night, while they were in the bed they shared at the joint condo. It took him three tries to say a full sentence, since he was recovering from a recent fight. His lung had been collapsed. Three ribs were cracked.

"I've been getting inquiries." She was naked beside him, resting on her belly, sipping from an extremely large glass of champagne.

"Inquiries are good."

"Not these ones. They're common criminals. Ordinary white-collar bullshit."

She appreciated that Fritz didn't ask her why she wasn't taking those cases. He was the first to understand that Hope needed work that was worthy of her time. "If you don't want to handle common criminals or ordinary white-collar bullshit, then what do you want?"

"I want names people recognize," Hope said. "Or crimes nasty enough that people will come to recognize the names of the criminals."

He rolled onto his back with only the faintest wince. He was naked aside from the bandages. "What should I do about it?"

The question touched her. Made her heart feel all soft and squishy. But it also, strangely, made her feel a little bit alarmed. "Nothing," she said. "Nothing at all."

"Good, because I can't breathe anyway. Probably won't be very useful for a week or two."

"That's fine. I don't need anything from you, professionally or otherwise."

He kissed the inside of her wrist. "You never do." And he actually sounded affectionate when he said it, not insulted.

Hope had expected Fritz would be more overbearing, more...well, more like the rest of the Friederlings. They were dynastic, imperialistic, like Genghis Khans of modern business. She'd thought that getting married into his family would mean that Fritz would force her to use all their resources. Even the nastier ones.

But he never crossed those lines. He was supportive, not aggressive.

It made Hope feel guilty.

The money kept dwindling, business remained quiet, and no interesting cases came through her door. Finances became grim. She wouldn't be able to last much longer without reaching into her husband's accounts to pay for her half of things—a trivial issue for him, but a deal breaker for her.

It wasn't until Hope's money ran out that she took a job far below her. A woman had been accused of murder, and not even an interesting one. She had allegedly shot her husband in a domestic dispute.

Hope was hired to represent the husband. The so-called victim of the crime. He was a vegetable with a bullet in his brain, and as far as Hope could tell, he completely deserved it. He was a batterer. He'd been tossing his wife into walls and slamming her head in the refrigerator for months before she finally snapped.

And Hope was defending the asshole who had smacked his wife around.

Boring. Unbefitting.

The defendant, Benita Morrice, was a sweet older woman. The story she told about her husband was heartbreaking. How he would get drunk and hit her. The daily fights. The constant gaslighting.

Benita's defense was good enough to present a real challenge. Hope didn't particularly care for trying to prosecute a victim of such violence, but it gave her something to do. Plus, rent was due, and at least Hope didn't have to deal with the husband directly. He wasn't capable of eating without a gastric tube, much less speaking in his defense.

Some weeks into the case, though, Hope got a strange feeling about Benita. Her answers were too good. She was too sympathetic.

And she was obviously lying about *something*.

Nobody was as sweet and sympathetic as Benita. Especially not in New York. Plus, when her husband asphyxiated to death in the hospital due to a supposed equipment failure, Benita looked very sad about it—sadder than anyone had a right to be about their abuser.

Hope didn't believe Benita's story anymore.

She hadn't used her powers of necrocognition to gather more information for a case before, but Benita Morrice was lying. And the only person who might know what she was lying about had already died.

Luckily, a client's death wasn't much of a deterrent for Hope.

DEADLY WRONG

She bribed a morgue attendant with a chunk of the retainer that Lewis Morrice's family paid her. She pulled the dead, abusive husband out of a refrigerator. And she asked him all the questions she hadn't been able to ask him while he was alive and comatose.

Lewis Morrice told a very different story than Benita. A story involving an affair on Benita's part, and how angry she'd been when he discovered it and demanded a divorce.

Benita had killed her husband so she could be with her lover.

The dead couldn't lie. If Lewis said that Benita had been throwing herself into walls and going to the hospital to document the fake abuse, then that was true. If he said that he found pictures of Benita in bed with another man, then that was also true.

And his claim that Benita had surprised him in the kitchen with a gun had to be true, too.

The dead couldn't lie.

But they also couldn't testify in court.

"What would you do about it?" she asked Fritz that weekend, after Lewis had been buried and Benita was about to walk free.

"Nothing," Fritz said. "The defendant is, what, sixty years old? She doesn't exactly present a public threat. Her only victim has already died and you can't bring him back to life. So I wouldn't do anything about it."

Hope glared at him. "If you had a soul, what would you do?"

He laughed. She wasn't sure if he thought she was joking or if he enjoyed pushing her buttons.

"Justice is complicated, Emmeline." He always called her by her middle name when he was trying to be cute. "Can justice be served when the victim has already died?"

"Benita Morrice isn't dead. She can still be punished."

"Then punish the murderer, but don't tell yourself that it will make anything better." Fritz poured a glass of wine for her, and when she took it, he rubbed his thumb over her knuckles. The lingering touch sent goosebumps cascading down her spine. "On the other hand, if you make an example of Benita Morrice, this could turn into exactly the kind of case you've always wanted."

Those words stuck in Hope's head: *Make an example of Benita Morrice.*

Fritz was right. There was nothing she could do to bring justice to Lewis Morrice.

But Hope could turn the case to her favor anyway.

So she had.

Hope tipped off the police. The case changed, and so did Hope's career.

And soon, all the newspapers in New York were printing Benita Morrice's name—with Hope Jimenez's alongside it.

Voices slid in and out of Isobel's periphery, making the memory ripple and disperse.

"Why isn't she waking up? It's been hours…"

"Adjusting to Hell is more difficult for some than others. It's especially difficult when the body is already weak."

"Strengthen her…bring her back…"

More memories swam around her, each one less distinct than the one before.

Isobel remembered dozens of Hope's cases. Once she had success talking to Lewis Morrice post-mortem, she started breaking more and more cases like that.

It was amazing how often people lied in court.

But if dead bodies were involved, nobody could lie to Hope Jimenez.

Isobel tumbled through the memories. She relived the heady thrills of increasing success, hiring new staff, bringing in partners to grow her business. She remembered when Fritz had a scrapbook of headlines sent to her for their first anniversary—all of them related to high-profile cases that she'd handled.

The jewelry and flowers and yachts and vacations were unimportant. That scrapbook was the most romantic gift he ever gave her.

They'd been married for a whole year, and that scrapbook was the moment that Hope realized that she really did love Fritz Friederling, and she might have even loved him from the moment he proposed to her on the *Friederling X*.

And then Ander had walked through her door again.

Just remembering him filled Isobel with a jolt of shock. Those catlike eyes, the well-fitted suit. They still terrified her.

She clawed her way toward consciousness, fleeing that meeting with Ander.

Isobel woke up in Hell.

CHAPTER SEVEN

WATER TRICKLED DOWN ISOBEL'S temple. She flinched away from it, trying to sit up.

A delicate hand touched her shoulder. "Don't move. It's okay. You're safe."

Isobel's vision cleared slowly. Blinking was hard—her eyelids felt like they had shriveled to raisins.

Once she could see, Isobel found a woman sitting at her bedside. Her face was touched by age lines though her skin was still firm, full breasts lifted by a corset dress. She was definitely human even though she dressed like a demon. Above the waist, her dress was little more than strips of leather connected to a snug collar. Voluminous black layers draped below the hips.

A gorgeous woman, all things considered, but she wasn't anyone that Isobel knew. The sight of her didn't even stir any of Hope's memories.

"Who are you?" Isobel finally asked.

"I'm the hostess for the Palace of Dis. My name is Ariane. I handle all the human visitors." She dipped a washcloth in a bowl of water and then stroked it over Isobel's forehead again. The cool moisture helped. It really did.

Isobel relaxed back against the pillows. She was in a room that looked like it had been carved from obsidian, though the decorations were as human as the woman taking care of her. It looked like everything had been ordered out of a catalogue.

"I'm thirsty," Isobel rasped.

"Of course you are." Ariane twisted the top off of a small water bottle and put it in Isobel's hand. "Drink slowly. We ration water here."

"Here...in Hell."

"Yes. The City of Dis."

Isobel dribbled the water over her lips. It tasted good but didn't make her feel much more hydrated. Like her soft tissues just didn't want to produce saliva now.

"If you're worried, your reaction to the transition between dimensions is completely normal," Ariane said, setting the bottle on the bedside table and standing. The corset pinched her waist to an impossibly narrow hourglass. "It's a bit of a shock for all of us. You'll adjust soon."

The door opened and Fritz entered. His face was flushed red. His clothes were rumpled, dust caught in his sleeves and lapels. It looked like he'd just been sandblasted. "How is she?" he asked Ariane.

"Ask her yourself, silly man." She swatted him lightly on the chest. Yet another woman who showed a little too much familiarity with Fritz. Isobel didn't find the strength to be remotely surprised about it. "How do you feel? Adjusting well?" She pulled his mouth open, peered into his eyes.

"I'm fine. It's not my first visit."

"Your first in months," Ariane said. "We've missed you. I don't think Isaac's found as fun a sparring partner in the interim."

Isobel gave Fritz a questioning look, which he ignored.

"I doubt Isaac's noticed. In any case, I'm not equal to sparring with kopides anymore." He hiked up the leg of his pants to reveal the prosthesis that had replaced one foot. He'd lost the appendage in a fight against a fallen angel. Fritz acted so normally that Isobel often forgot about it.

"If that's slowing you down, then it's because you've succumbed to the Friederling curse, not because you're missing a foot. You're driving hard for money and power rather than training as much as you should." Ariane tweaked the collar of his shirt. "Look at you. Wearing a suit and everything. And working with the Union? What would Grandpa Friederling think?"

Fritz's eye twitched. "I need to speak to Judge Abraxas."

Ariane's hands dropped, toying with the belt on her bodice. "Is that so?"

"As soon as possible. I'm told that you're helping make appointments with him these days."

"Sometimes," Ariane said.

She was edging away from Fritz now, moving toward the door.

He caught her wrist. "It's urgent, Ariane."

"It's always urgent. This is Hell. Everything is

life and death." The playful teasing had vanished from her tone. "What do you need?"

"Contract dissolution. Easy enough for the resident Judge," Fritz said. "Shouldn't take more than a few minutes of his time."

Ariane's lips thinned. She glanced at Isobel, then back to Fritz. "Minutes may be too much when his seconds are so valuable."

"Just tell him. Abraxas knows me. He'd give me hours if I needed it."

"I can't make guarantees," she said, and then she was gone, vanishing from the room without so much as a hint of promise.

Fritz looked tempted to follow her, but he settled for removing his jacket, hanging it on a hook by the door. Apparently, the unsettlingly normal-looking bedroom in Hell belonged to him.

"That sounds bad," Isobel said.

"Ariane's flighty and useless. Don't worry about her." Fritz raked his hands through his hair, shaking orange dust out of his blond locks. "How do you feel?"

"Like a magical contract is beating my ass," she said, grimacing as she got out of bed. "Every time I fall asleep…" She bit off the rest of her response. She wasn't ready to discuss what she'd been remembering.

"Abraxas will see us," Fritz said firmly. "And he'll do it quickly. He has a standing relationship with my family. He owes us, in fact. As long as that idiot woman gets to him quickly enough…"

"Six days," Isobel said.

"It'll only take a few minutes, as I said. Don't

worry about the time." Fritz shot a look at the wall. "It's closer to five days now, though."

His clock was divided into seven sections, measuring time by the days on Earth rather than hours.

Isobel's heart plummeted. It had felt like she had slept for a long time—a full night of rest, at the very least. But a full night of rest in Dis meant losing a lot more time on Earth.

She wondered if Cèsar had noticed that Fritz was gone yet.

"What am I supposed to do now?" Isobel asked. "I can't wait for this Abraxas guy to decide he's ready to see us. I'm running out of time. I have to *do* something."

Fritz arched an eyebrow. "Well, then…how about a tour?"

Fritz led Isobel through the Palace. The whole compound sort of looked like Tim Burton's medieval nightmare, with all its spiked portcullises and spindly towers, though she could barely make out its shape against the darkness of the city beyond. Everything was shadows against shadows, layers of darkness cloaked in smoke.

His room had been in one of the central buildings. It was connected to the others by narrow bridges with frail railings that she felt might snap if she leaned on them.

The instant they stepped onto one of those bridges, Isobel was grateful for the leather outfit that Fritz had given her. The hot wind battered at her exposed flesh. If she'd had any more skin showing, she might have been flayed.

"Take advantage of the local fashion," Fritz shouted over the wind, handing a bundle of black veils to her.

Isobel wrapped them around her head as he hiked his jacket up around his ears again. She covered her nose, mouth, and hair, leaving only a narrow eye slit. The wind tried to jerk the veils away from her. She clutched them tightly under her jaw.

"This is awful," Isobel said. She had to yell back at him to be able to hear her own voice. "Is it always like this?"

"It's Hell. What do you think?"

Fritz walked briskly toward the next tower, hanging on to the railing as though he weren't at all concerned by its apparent fragility. His suit whipped around him. He'd only put a few steps between them when the gusting smoke and dust made him difficult to see.

Isobel hurried to keep up, but she kept catching herself stopping to stare beyond the Palace battlements.

The City of Dis, as seen from the bridge, was the darkest, most miserable place that Isobel recalled ever being in her life. That said a lot. She had lived for months in curtained isolation within Ander's house, and then months more in Helltown. Isobel knew dark, miserable places.

Everything was much more industrial than she'd expected. Half of the buildings she could see were belching sticky black smoke into the air to be jerked away on the wind, which smelled of human meat. Judging by the faint flicker of gaslight, the outlying neighborhoods climbed all the way into the mountains, which were a cruel black line etched against the crimson sky.

The streets looked like they were seething, too. It was hard to tell. She was very high, and the air was very clogged, and everything was so dark.

Isobel didn't mind demons. The quality of their company and trustworthiness were as variable as with any human. A lot of them were terrible, but then, so were mortals. The fact that demons tended to have a taste for flesh, violence, and chaos wasn't a big deal.

But an entire city of them—an entire city of hellborn, just like Ander...

If she fell off the bridge, she might drown in the misery of that city.

Fritz was halfway to the next tower now. She fixed her eyes to the bridge and picked up her pace. Her choppy breaths were hot against her face, trapped within the veils.

Entering the opposite tower was a relief. The air felt a thousand times more breathable. Isobel ripped the veils down and sucked in a long gasp of it.

"You'll get used to it," Fritz said, shaking sand off of his jacket. "It's not too bad inside. I just wish they'd cover the bridges."

She followed him down the spiral stairs. "Why don't they?"

"I think they like to keep the humans a little uncomfortable." He spoke in a low voice. This tower was more populous than the others, and not just with humans—Isobel had never seen so much variety in demons before, despite her time in Helltown.

Many of the creatures they passed on their way down the stairs would have never passed for human. The differences weren't superficial, like Isobel frequently saw on Earth—discolored skin and horns, for instance. There were insect-like bodies, too many legs, things that slithered.

She tried to keep her gaze on Fritz. If she'd learned anything as a Helltown priestess, it was that demons didn't appreciate staring.

But she looked at them really hard out of the corner of her eye.

"This tower is open to the public," Fritz said. "There are a couple of temples scattered throughout the levels, some study rooms, a bingo lounge—"

Her bark of laughter interrupted him. "Bingo?"

"Everyone likes bingo," Fritz said.

"And I thought the karaoke halls in Helltown were funny."

"This administration banned karaoke in the Palace years ago. There's nothing worse than a warbling chisav drunk on human blood. Are you hungry?"

The sudden change in subject threw Isobel.

She wasn't really hungry. She couldn't remember the last time she'd been hungry. It felt like she hadn't digested any of the cinnamon buns that she'd eaten so long ago. "Sure, we can eat," Isobel said. Better than admitting that she might have become too dead to get hungry.

Fritz pushed a pair of tall double doors open. They were adorned with horns and sparkling obsidian. The handles looked like fangs. A very intimidating entrance.

The other side was somewhat less intimidating.

It was a café.

She wasn't surprised, not exactly. She'd been to cafés in Helltown. There was even a very cute bed and breakfast that was favored by visitors who had just arrived from Dis.

But this one looked so...normal. Any of those little round tables could have been found at a Starbucks on Earth. The line for coffee wrapped all along the wall, which was decorated with photographs of coffee cups and people harvesting beans. It even smelled like a Starbucks.

There were tables out on the balconies overlooking the Palace courtyard, but nobody was sitting in the sandstorm. Surprise, surprise.

"We'll have to skip the espresso, unless you want to spend all afternoon in line," Fritz said.

An entire afternoon in Hell could have been days on Earth. She shook her head. "No coffee. Thanks."

Fritz grabbed a couple of pastries out of a glass case using a pair of tongs—which were, apparently, free for visitors to the Palace—and set them down at a table.

Isobel couldn't remember a time that a chocolate croissant wouldn't have sounded good to her, but now the sight of it filled her mouth with the taste of ash. "I'd rather not spend any time here at all," Isobel said. "We need to be doing something. Talking to people, finding that Ariane woman…"

"We have a few minutes," Fritz said.

He pushed the croissant toward her on a plate.

Isobel took it, but she didn't try to take a bite.

A woman broke away from the head of the coffee line, approaching their table with a mug cupped between her hands. Isobel hadn't seen Ariane enter. Apparently, the hostess who took care of everyone in the Palace didn't have to wait for her java fix like everyone else did.

"I have news," Ariane said, offering the cup to Isobel.

After a moment's hesitation, she took it. She wasn't hungry, but she was still so thirsty.

"Is your news the good kind, or the kind that I don't want to hear?" Fritz asked.

Ariane smiled wanly. "I'm not sure."

"I probably don't want to hear it, then."

"It's not for you." Ariane turned to Isobel. "You're wanted in the Library."

Surprise jolted through her. "I am?"

"A librarian has requested your presence. It's an honor, in a way. They don't talk to many people."

The fact that it was only an honor "in a way" made Isobel suspect it wasn't an honor at all, but something much more dangerous. She looked to Fritz for guidance over the rim of the coffee cup as she took a long, slow sip. His glower didn't make her feel any better.

"I wouldn't make them wait very long," Ariane

added. "The librarians are special."

"We'll visit if we have the time," Fritz said. "There isn't much of that to go around right now, unfortunately." He was lying. He had no intent of taking Isobel to the Library. She could tell by how stiff he had become.

Ariane seemed satisfied, though. "Off to court," she said with an apologetic smile. "Always so much to do here."

Fritz scowled at her retreating back.

Isobel set the cup down with a hard *thump*. "You didn't ask about Judge Abraxas. Are you giving up?"

"Never," Fritz said. He took her coffee and sipped it. Fine with Isobel. The drink hadn't sated her horrible thirst at all.

He still looked pretty comfortable in the café, like he was waiting for something. If they were going to sit around, then Isobel was going to ask questions. She deserved the answers. "Lucrezia," she said.

Fritz heaved a sigh. "You and I weren't monogamous, Belle. We agreed that we'd continue to have affairs whenever we wanted after we got married. Lucrezia was one of those affairs for me."

"Let me get this straight." Isobel massaged her temples with her fingertips, as though she could smooth the flow of memories through her skull. "When we were married, we lived apart, didn't get involved in each others' business, and saw other people freely."

"That's right."

It would explain why she didn't remember

feeling jealous, but… "Didn't our marriage mean *anything*?"

Fritz's lips pinched. "Yes. It did."

She gazed at him in the light of Hell, trying to see a man that she would have married with no strings attached. He was attractive. He'd always been attractive. And there was that scrapbook he'd made to commemorate the growing success of her career as lawyer… Just thinking about it still made her heart do funny flip-flops.

But that wasn't enough, was it? Marrying a hot guy who knew how to be nice?

Isobel wasn't even in a relationship with Cèsar and the thought of him running off with another woman was sickening. Damn it all, but he was so *charming*. She didn't want anyone else touching his nicely shaped ass. Especially that partner of his at the OPA.

Isobel Stonecrow was confident about at least two things where her personality was concerned: she enjoyed baking cookies much more than being skinny, and she was a very jealous woman. Not crazy jealous, but a healthy, rational level of jealous. She liked her men to only have eyes for her.

Was that so odd?

Yet she had, apparently, married a man who had no intent of remaining monogamous.

Isobel watched the slow line of people moving past the counter, attended by a petite barista with horns curlier than a ram's. She couldn't bring herself to look at Fritz and know that he'd probably fucked that bridesmaid on their honeymoon.

"I just don't get it," she finally said. "Open

marriage. I don't get it."

"Most people wouldn't. It makes sense to us, and that's what matters." Fritz picked his bagel apart. "Well, it used to make sense to us."

Why the hell had she married him?

She remembered meeting him and the actual wedding, but everything between was still a shadowy blur. "How did you propose to me?" Isobel asked. "Was it when I graduated law school?"

That pinched look relaxed a fraction. "You remember."

She almost did. If she thought hard about it, she could almost peel back the veil of memory to a yacht swaying on the ocean, a cheap ring bought in some Caribbean port, a few drunken exchanges. Mostly, Isobel remembered that they'd been having fun.

She found it hard to believe that she would have married someone just for fun.

On the other hand, she was learning a lot about Hope Jimenez that was hard to believe.

"Our relationship was unique," Fritz said. "But never doubt that I loved Hope, my Emmeline, more than any other man has loved a woman. I hope you remember that soon." The silence that followed his pronouncement was ominous.

He was hoping that she'd remember soon enough for it to matter. While she still had a body. While she was still almost alive.

Their awkward silence was broken when a handsome young man, probably in his early twenties, dropped into a chair across from Fritz.

"Ramelan!" Fritz shook his hand enthusiastically.

"Friederling," Ramelan said with no small amount of affection. He had a strong accent that Isobel couldn't place. "I didn't expect to hear from you again after our last encounter. Most of the men I fought have avoided me ever since!"

"Being bested is nothing personal. You're a better fighter than me. You earned the title."

"I broke your collarbone earning that title," Ramelan said.

"It's fine now," Fritz said, tapping his fingers over the bone. He turned to Isobel. "Kopides like Ramelan and me get together every few years to see who's the best via a tournament. It's sort of medieval, but it's a great honor to be considered the greatest kopis."

"It's not every few years. It's whenever the last greatest kopis dies," the young man interjected.

"Yes, that. Ramelan took over four years ago on Earth." Fritz smiled wryly. "It's probably better that he won. I wouldn't have liked all the ceremonial duties. And having to spend so much time in the Palace of Dis…"

"It's not so bad." Ramelan took one of Isobel's hands in both of his. "You—you are much too beautiful to be in the Palace of Dis. You don't belong here. Let me take you back to the portal to Earth before this place turns you into a husk."

Isobel removed her hand from his. Sure, he was handsome, but she must have been almost a decade older than him. He was so damn *young*.

Cute, though. Very cute.

"Actually, this is the woman I told you about," Fritz said, pulling his bagel into eighths. He hadn't actually eaten any of it. The crumbs were scattered across his plate.

Ramelan let out a sigh. "Ah. *That* woman."

"And what exactly did he tell you about me?" Isobel tried not to sound too accusatory.

The greatest kopis put a finger to his lips and shook his head. When he lifted his hand, his sleeve slipped down his arm, exposing a series of tattoos on the inside of his wrist. Each of them was small, no bigger than a thumbnail. They weren't any kind of runes Isobel recognized.

"If you're done?" Ramelan prompted.

Fritz pushed the bagel away from himself. "Whenever you are."

CHAPTER EIGHT

RAMELAN WALKED ALMOST TOO quickly for Isobel to keep up with him. She had to scurry to avoid being left behind in the labyrinthine corridors of the Palace of Dis.

All windows vanished about halfway down the tower, and she lost count of the floors after a few more flights. But she had the distinct sense that they had gone underground at some point. The silence was much too weighty. The corridors became narrower. The air warmed.

An elevator appeared at the end of the hall. It was a rickety metal cage, and its floor didn't quite align with the tile they were standing on, so Isobel could see the greasy pistons underneath. Steam hissed from the gap.

The lift was entirely mechanical.

Actually, Isobel hadn't seen anything with electronic components since getting into Hell. The clocks all had exposed cogs, the elevator was steam-powered, and even the coffee had been manually brewed in the kitchen.

"Here it is," Ramelan said, opening the gate

and stepping aside so Fritz and Isobel could get in. "Electricity, as you can see, doesn't work in Hell."

"It doesn't work reliably in Helltown either," Isobel said. Ramelan looked askance at her. "It's this neighborhood in Los Angeles where demons live."

"An undercity," he said.

Fritz led Isobel into the elevator. "No, it's on the surface."

Ramelan shut the doors and pushed a lever down. "The demons have colonized a surface neighborhood?" He looked thoughtful as the elevator groaned, hissed, and began to descend. "That's going to be a problem. I'm surprised you're allowing it."

"We have plans for that," Fritz said.

That was news to Isobel. "You do?"

"The Union does. Don't worry about it."

She was going to have to worry about it. She had friends in Helltown. If the Union was planning to invade—well, she might not survive to see it. Isobel couldn't think about that yet. She pushed it out of her mind.

"I've wanted to talk to you about them. The Union won't leave me alone," Ramelan said. "They want me to work for their organization."

"Who can blame them? You're the greatest kopis. You're potentially a very valuable asset," Fritz said.

"I'm a man. I'm not an asset. Will you remind Lucrezia di Angelis of that fact?"

"Frankly, my friend, I don't think that my advocacy on your behalf would help all that much."

"What good is being director for an evil organization if not for the leverage, eh?" Ramelan asked.

"The health insurance is pretty good," Fritz said, totally straight-faced.

The elevator only dropped a few levels before stopping again.

Ramelan pushed his sleeve up, exposing the tattoos that Isobel had glimpsed on the inside of his wrist. "They're keys," he explained, waving his arm in front of the controls for the elevator. It began moving again.

"You've got access to more of the Palace than I expected," Fritz remarked.

Ramelan winked. "Lucky for you."

The lift finally stopped at the very bottom level. When the cage opened, Isobel was facing a dark, windowless hallway painted with murals. Judging by how flaky and discolored the paint was, those murals were probably centuries old, and they depicted fights between demons and angels. The demons looked to be winning.

The door at the end of the hallway was as intimidating as the one to the café. Ramelan waved his tattooed wrist in front of it. The lock inside clicked, muffled by several inches of heavy stone.

He pushed it open a few inches then stepped back. "I have to live and train in this place. I don't want the Judge to see me."

"Understood. We appreciate your help," Fritz said.

"I'm a very valuable asset. Aren't I?" Ramelan

gave Isobel a ghost of a smile that lacked his earlier confidence, then retreated down the hallway the way he had come.

Isobel watched him go, feeling a little bit lost.

It finally sank in where they had gone: Ramelan had escorted them to the court where the Judge worked.

Ariane hadn't arranged a meeting, but they were going to meet him anyway.

"Foreboding" wasn't a strong enough word for what was creeping over Isobel. More like "sheer, panicky dread."

"Is Judge Abraxas dangerous?" she asked, trying to gather her confidence. She couldn't seem to find it.

"Yes, incredibly dangerous."

And with those words of confidence, Fritz stepped through the door.

Stepping into a courtroom used to be exhilarating for Hope Jimenez. It had made her giddy every time, knowing what she was about to do, knowing the power that she held over what would happen in that hallowed room.

The excitement had faded not long after she left law school. You could only see so many courtrooms before they started to become boring.

Stepping into the Judge's domain, Isobel felt exhilarated again. Her pulse throbbed in her temples. Her drying skin was hot.

It wasn't the excitement of a lawyer in control. It was the adrenaline of facing the infernal unknown.

Worse, the courtroom didn't look anything like they did on Earth. The room was a literal pit. Stands rimmed the room, looking down on a central rune that marked the floor. Isobel knew enough about magic to be able to identify a protection ward. It wasn't too dissimilar from some of the ones that she'd seen at the Los Angeles OPA offices.

There were no witnesses, no jury, no lawyers. All of those curved benches were empty. There were torches mounted on the walls.

This looked less like a place where justice was served and more like somewhere that the Inquisition might have happened.

Fritz's face was so close in the darkness. It startled her to see how many lines he had at the corners of his eyes now. Not that he was looking old—not at all. But older than the man Hope Jimenez had married. "Hang out here for a minute. We'll go down between cases and speak with the Judge."

Between cases?

She looked down again. She had been so overwhelmed by the room itself that she hadn't noticed a demon crouching in the center of the glowing protection rune. He was skinny and pale. Maybe a nightmare.

Another demon looked down on him from the stand. It was a tall, broad-shouldered creature engulfed in velvety red robes that hid everything from his hands to his face. The only distinguishing feature about him was his height. Aside from that, there could have been anything lurking in the dark depths of his hood—another one of those horned demons, or an unusually tall nightmare, or something that Isobel had never seen before.

She was willing to bet on the latter.

Isobel assumed that this was the "incredibly dangerous" Judge Abraxas.

"Death," said the Judge.

"No," whispered the nightmare. "No, please."

Ariane swept from the shadows behind the stand, the train of her black dress dragging on the floor. "The verdict is death," she said, louder than the Judge. With a twist of her wrist, the rune on the floor flared.

Leather-clad guards seized the nightmare by the arms and dragged him into a dark passage. He sobbed all the way down, voice echoing into the empty courtroom.

The Judge settled his hand briefly on Ariane's shoulder. He had white skin that reminded Isobel of boneyards.

So at least parts of him resembled a human.

"Next, Ariane." Even though he spoke softly, his voice was amplified throughout the entire room. There was something eerily intimate in the way that he spoke to the beautiful witch. That was the tone of a man who thought nobody else was listening, who was speaking to someone that he knew much better than a judge should know his employee.

She brushed her fingers over his—the barest touch of skin against skin. Then she descended into the pit to operate the rune again.

"Now," Fritz said, moving to climb down the stands.

Before he made it two levels down, a door opposite the one the nightmare had been dragged through opened.

Lucrezia di Angelis stepped into the courtroom.

Fritz dropped back to his knees and pulled Isobel down with him, swearing under his breath.

"*You're* not on trial," the Judge said, his hood turning so that he could survey the woman critically. "At the very least, you're not on my schedule. What are you doing in these hallowed walls?"

Ariane frowned. "I'm sorry. I'll have her removed."

He lifted a hand to stop her. "That won't be necessary. The fact that Lucrezia di Angelis has come here suggests that it must be important."

"Well, I don't know about that. Important enough, I suppose." Lucrezia's mouth twisted with distaste. "Have you spoken with Fritz Friederling yet?"

The Judge was silent for so long that Isobel wasn't sure that he'd heard her speak at all. "Fritz Friederling," he finally said. "I don't know this man."

For once, Fritz's reputation hadn't preceded him. Bad timing for that.

Fritz looked shocked, though. The blood had drained from his face. "Didn't you say that Judge Abraxas owes your family a favor?" Isobel whispered under her breath. Even those soft words were amplified within the court, though it didn't seem to reach the floor.

He nodded mutely.

Lucrezia was speaking again. "He's running around with a zombie or…something." She rolled her eyes. "What he's doing is of no interest to you or the Palace. However, I'm certain he's breaking several laws relevant to my job on Earth. I want him turned over to my custody."

"Zombie?" The Judge almost sounded amused.

"He seems to have resurrected his dead wife. Nothing illegal by the laws of Hell, I'm afraid."

The muscles in Isobel's shoulders knotted until it felt like they might rip her spine in half. Lucrezia sounded so damn *dismissive*. "What's crawled up her ass?" Isobel muttered.

Fritz leaned in close to her hear. "It's funny how you fuck a woman a few times and she thinks you're in a relationship."

"*Funny?*"

"Friederling, Friederling," the Judge mused aloud. "Where have I heard that name?"

Lucrezia paced, white heels clicking against the floor. "Lord only knows. He has a way of making trouble."

"The summit," Ariane said. "He's on the list."

"Ah. Fritz Friederling is involved in the organization of the Union's semi-centennial summit. That's right." The Judge's hood swiveled to face Lucrezia again. Even though Isobel couldn't see his eyes, she thought that she would have shriveled under the weight of his invisible gaze. "You wouldn't get into a fight with someone who might interfere with the plans for this summit, would you?"

"He's a bit player," Lucrezia said. "Meaningless to the grander scheme of things."

"He is attending, though."

"Yes. He's attending. Everyone's attending. It doesn't change anything. Fritz Friederling has broken the Union's rules by maintaining a portal to Hell in his private residence, dragging a pet zombie around, and being a general nuisance. Now he's in the Palace. I want him in my custody."

Pet zombie? Isobel's hackles lifted.

Fritz rose, tugging on his suit jacket to straighten it, squaring his shoulders. He was preparing to do battle.

"What are you doing?" Isobel hissed, grabbing his hem.

He ignored her and moved down the stairs. "I have to object to that assessment." He spoke just loudly enough that it carried throughout the entire courtroom.

Everyone looked up to see Fritz and Isobel in the stands.

Ariane slapped her hand over her face. "You stupid man," she whispered. It carried through the court.

Lucrezia tensed. "Friederling." Her eyes flicked to Isobel. "And Hope."

"I haven't broken a single rule for the Office of Preternatural Affairs or its Union division," Fritz said.

"Maintaining private artifacts that are so powerful is a rule violation."

"The portal belongs to the Friederlings. It's not

my personal property, and even if it were, those rules don't apply to anything employees own prior to employment. Also, if you checked my file, you'd see I have the portal registered in the database—among other things."

"And I'm not a pet zombie," Isobel added. She didn't really want anyone paying attention to her, but she couldn't leave that alone.

"Pet zombie, sex toy, it doesn't matter," Lucrezia said. "We've been bringing the hammer down on necromancy and an OPA director should know better than to drag that walking violation around with you!"

"She's a very well-preserved zombie," the Judge said. He was leaning back in his chair now, hooded head resting on his knuckles. Isobel thought his posture almost looked amused by the argument unfolding in his courtroom, but it was hard to tell.

"This woman is not a zombie," Fritz said. "She's the product of a contract with Ander."

"Ander is a well-known slaver," Ariane filled in when the Judge didn't react. There was new sympathy in her eyes when she studied Isobel. "He's best known for employing people on the brink of death and restoring them to life. A rare demon with somewhat necromantic powers."

"Interesting," the Judge said. "Useful."

"He's dead now," Fritz said.

Understanding flitted over Ariane's features. "And her contract is expiring. How long?"

"A matter of days now. I need you to nullify the contract, Judge Abraxas." Fritz reached into his jacket, extracting a slender envelope.

"Why should I help you?" the Judge asked.

"I'm a Friederling." He said it like it should be significant.

But Judge Abraxas didn't react. "You want this contract nullified. Lucrezia wants your blood. Court is always tedious, but dragging your mortal dramas into it has rendered it more of a chore than normal."

Fritz crossed the warded floor to set the envelope on the Judge's stand. "The terms of your treaty with the House of Belial says that you have to nullify this for me."

"What a joke! You don't care about any of this, Judge," Lucrezia said. "You know you don't. But you're the authority in this Palace, and you need to give me permission to arrest this man within your walls. All you have to do is say the word. I will make this chore vanish."

"You're right, Lucrezia di Angelis," Judge Abraxas said. "I've no interest in your affairs. They're meaningless to this court. I won't turn him over to your custody, but I'll have nothing to do with his zombie's contract problems, either."

Anger crackled in the air surrounding Fritz. "But—Judge Abraxas—"

The *crack* of the gavel on the podium interrupted him.

"You intruded on my court against my wishes," the Judge said. "You'll be incarcerated in the cells until I decide if I want to do anything else with you."

"*Incarcerated?*"

"The verdict is temporary incarceration in the cells," Ariane announced, the same way that she had announced the verdict for the demon that had been on trial earlier.

Summoned by her voice, a pair of demons guards limped into the room. They moved awkwardly because they had no necks; their heads were sunken into their chests, and their mouths formed toothed, gaping holes in their stomachs.

Fritz didn't fight them when they pulled his wrists behind his back, binding them with a rope.

"Stop that!" Isobel snapped.

They didn't listen to her.

If only she remembered her time as Hope Jimenez better—the lawyer would have known what to do. She would have had some genius idea for intervening and convincing Judge Abraxas to listen to her.

Instead, she could only gape as demons dragged Fritz Friederling away, taking him to cells that could have been anywhere, as far as she knew.

He looked infuriated, but he still didn't fight.

She'd seen him take on more than two demons before. He could have killed them. He could have broken free. "Fritz," she said. He shook his head silently at her before they made him disappear through those doors.

Lucrezia looked almost as angry as Isobel felt. She rounded on Judge Abraxas. "Then what about *her*?" She jabbed a finger at Isobel.

The Judge studied Isobel for a long time. Too long. She felt like she was trapped under the weight of his scrutiny for endless days.

"Meaningless," he said decisively. And then he turned from her as though he'd already forgotten that she was in the room. "Next, Ariane."

CHAPTER NINE

MEANINGLESS.

THAT WAS ONE hell of a verdict for a judge to hand down to Isobel.

She used to be one of the best lawyers in New York. There were a lot of newspaper articles and enraged blogs to attest to that. Now she was a necrocognitive with enough of a reputation to attract clients all over the West Coast. She was good at what she did. She had been good at what she used to do.

Isobel wasn't meaningless.

The way that he had said that made her feel cold and sick all over.

Ariane escorted her to the upper levels of the Palace, and Isobel followed her numbly, watching the silhouette of the woman's black dress swaying against the black stone walls.

The hostess dropped her off at a lobby on the ground level. "They won't keep Fritz for long," Ariane said, rubbing Isobel's shoulders in a gesture that was probably meant to be comforting. "There's no reason to waste resources containing him. He'll be out within the week."

Isobel wasn't sure if Ariane meant a week in Dis time or Earth time. It was a pretty big difference.

Of course, it didn't seem all that important, considering that the huge clock built into the wall of the lobby was ticking all too quickly toward the expiration of Isobel's contract.

"This was supposed to save my life," she said. "Judge Abraxas should have been able to help me."

Ariane squeezed Isobel's arms gently. "The Palace Library is that way." She nodded toward a door leading out to the courtyard. "If you follow the path beyond the flesh gardens, you'll find the door." The hostess left again, probably heading back downstairs for more time in court with Judge Abraxas.

The Library?

It took Isobel a moment to remember that one of the librarians wanted to speak with her. Fritz had dismissed it so quickly that Isobel hadn't given the request much consideration.

Now that Fritz was trapped in a cell and the Judge had refused their plea, it seemed that she had time to visit.

What harm could it do?

Isobel stepped outside, into the courtyard. The soil was hard packed and red, as though iron-rich blood infused its every grain. Spiked battlements reared high overhead. There were guards patrolling the walls, some nightmares and some of those beasts with the mouths in their chests, but none of them looked at her twice.

She was far from the only human walking around the Palace. People were strolling along the black stone paths, sheltered from the worst of the dust and wind.

Even though she kept her eyes to the path, she couldn't help but wonder what had led so many people—and many of them dressed in expensive suits—to live or work in Hell. Such a dark, miserable place had to have some redeeming quality to make it worthwhile.

Isobel would bet it was money. It was usually money.

The Library inhabited the entire bottom half of a nearby tower. The floor was some kind of semi-translucent glass or crystal covered in desks occupied by orange-robed demons.

A single spiral staircase led into the stacks above Isobel. There must have been tens of thousands of books up there—more books than anyone could read in two or three lifetimes.

Definitely more than she'd ever be able to read in what remained of her lifetime.

Once Isobel was inside the Library of Dis, she wasn't sure what to do with herself. People were climbing the stairs, perusing the stacks, talking to the demons at the desks. Nobody greeted her. No guards tried to turn her away.

Isobel approached one of the nightmare guards by the doors. "Excuse me," she said, ignoring the familiar surge of fear that accompanied close proximity to a nightmare demon. "I was told a librarian here wanted to speak with me."

The demon gave her a once-over. "What's a

librarian want with a dead girl?"

Nobody had ever recognized her as anything but living before, but apparently the contract's magic had faded enough that she looked like a zombie now. That didn't do favorable things for her ego. "I don't know what the librarian wants. Where do I find them?"

"You already have," the nightmare said, jerking his chin toward the robed demons.

There were dozens of them. Isobel didn't know where to start.

"Thanks," she said.

He grabbed her arm before she could move away. His nostrils flared as he inhaled. "You're terrified." Isobel tried to pull free, but he was holding too tight. "Who owns you? I want a taste."

"The Hand of Death," Isobel said. "I'm a priestess. You can't touch me."

That worked in Helltown as a way to get most demons to leave her alone. In Dis, it wasn't nearly as effective.

The nightmare pulled her to him, looping an arm around her waist. "I'm off my shift in a few minutes," he murmured, scraping skeletal fingers down her throat.

Her skin crawled like it was going to peel off her body and go hide in the dark courtroom.

Isobel could fight back. She'd handled worse demons than this *thing*, even if it were strengthened by being in Hell. But she couldn't guarantee that she'd break free without damaging herself permanently.

"Release her, Antoine," said a gravelly voice

behind Isobel.

Isobel twisted. Her savior looked very much like a goat walking on its hind legs, though the hands that protruded from the ends of her sleeves were those of a human child. Her long muzzle was covered in coarse fur. Her eyes were framed by thick eyelashes, and the pupils were ovals.

The nightmare released Isobel and stepped back, bowing his head respectfully. "Sorry."

"Thanks," Isobel said to the goat, trying to slow her pounding heart.

"I'm the librarian who summoned you, Isobel Stonecrow." When she spoke, her lips moved as fluidly as a human's. The teeth that flashed were square and yellow. "I've heard of your trouble. I can't nullify your contract, but I can rewrite it."

"What? Really? How can you rewrite my contract?" Isobel asked. Maybe her friend Ann hadn't been that far off about needing a magical lawyer after all.

"Come to my desk." The goat limped across the crystal floor, and Isobel followed.

They stopped at a tidy desk covered by two stacks of parchment. It didn't look like the paper had been made from trees; it was too rough, too pinkish. Death tingled very faintly around it.

That parchment had been made from skin.

The goat demon settled herself on a stool, then gestured to the opposite chair. "Sit." Isobel obeyed quickly. "I'm Onoskelis, a librarian. All documents in the Palace fall under my authority. Your contract is currently owned by a human man but resides inside the Palace battlements, which means I can modify it."

"I'm sorry. I'm not familiar with the Palace's rules, or what the librarians here are like, but… that's not something librarians can do where I come from. Modifying contracts."

Onoskelis's liquid eyes sparked. "I'm not merely a librarian in this Palace. I am a very special type of librarian. My coworkers and I are different from every other demon dwelling in Hell."

"It just sounds too good to be true," Isobel said.

The librarian set the page she was writing on aside, licked her fingers, and peeled a fresh piece of parchment away from the stack. "I'll prove it to you." She wrote a few short lines and pushed it toward Isobel, along with the pen. "Sign this."

It was a revision to her contract—the one that she had signed for Ander. And it returned most of her memories as Hope Jimenez.

Isobel took the pen, but hesitated.

She had signed those memories away for a reason. The odds that she wouldn't like what she remembered were high.

But in order to get rid of that contract, she was going to have to remember at some point. She couldn't keep running forever.

Isobel held her breath and signed the revision.

The ink sank into the page, quickly growing dull.

For an instant, nothing else happened. Isobel dropped the pen. She opened her mouth to complain.

Then her mind split open and memories came pouring back.

Hope Jimenez sat in a shadowy office with a briefcase in her lap and a stack of papers on the desk in front of her. Isobel recognized the office—not from Hope's memories, but from ones much more recent than that.

It was Ander's office at his home in Hell.

Hope Jimenez didn't belong there.

Yet Onoskelis's contract had definitely brought the memory of Ander's office forth, and she was definitely still Hope Jimenez, judging by the tailored suit she wore and the slenderness of her thighs.

She wasn't alone in that office. Ander lounged beside her, cigar caught between his teeth. "Of course I've got another one for you. I'll always have another one for *you*, my dear girl." He had the charm turned up to eleven. He was in a good mood.

"I can't take any more of your referrals," Hope said.

Ander's cigar drooped. "Why not?"

"Do you think that I'm oblivious, Ander? I know what you've been doing with the information I give you."

It had been three years since Benita Morrice had killed her husband. The Morrice murder had definitely been a career-maker for Hope. People had been seeking her out since it got splashed all over the news—but not with the kind of cases she wanted to do.

Ander had been one of those people who

sought her out. He wanted to make a deal. He would exchange client referrals for information garnered from Hope's unique ability to speak with the dead.

The demon knew CEOs, actors, and politicians —some of who were simply humans who had gotten tangled up in demon affairs, but a surprising number of which were secretly demons themselves.

They were always in trouble. He had kept her chin-deep in work for months.

It was wonderful. Hope was rich without help from the Friederling fortune. And she was quickly getting to be as famous as anyone she represented.

The problem was the price of it all. Ander was doing things with the information that Hope gave him. Bad things. Things that she wasn't comfortable with at all, and things that even Fritz probably would have disapproved of if he knew anything about them.

Too bad she couldn't ask his opinion, since Fritz still had no idea that Hope was working with Ander.

"Who cares what I do with your information, my dear?" Ander asked. "You don't know any of these people. And they're all certainly bad people, entirely deserving of whatever comes to them."

She toyed with the buckle on her briefcase, twisting and untwisting the gold latch. "It's the principle of the thing." She couldn't bring herself to say that she just didn't imagine herself as someone who helped demons kill people, no matter how profitable it was.

Of course, that was exactly what she had been

doing. Hope had given Ander information to help him find the Grimaldi family five days earlier. And then, two days after that, the entire family had been found dead in a cornfield.

That wasn't the first time that Hope's necrocognition had led to deaths, but it was the first time she hadn't been able to ignore it. The Grimaldi family was a big deal. The murders had been so messy that they had been given the front page of the newspaper, above the fold, where anyone who might buy a copy on a street corner could see their portraits.

The article about the Grimaldis had bumped Hope's latest case to a slender column on the second page.

Once she saw that, she had resolved to end her deal with Ander, whatever it took.

But her resolve was fading now that Ander was gazing at her with his pathetic, catlike eyes and the drooping cigar. It was like she'd kicked his favorite puppy. "What will you do for money? The size of your current business is only because of everything I've given you."

"I've worked for the current size of my business," she corrected. "We've made exchanges, and you 'gave' me nothing. Everything has been quid pro quo."

That got the corner of his mouth twitching. Not quite a smile, but he had to fight it. "You've always been my favorite, Hope," Ander said. "You'll always be my favorite."

"Then you understand why I don't want to take part in the more murderous parts of your business."

"But *Hope*."

"No, Ander. That's not how I work."

"Does that mean you're not going to sign with me now, either? Darling Hope, after all we've been through together, after everything that we've accomplished…"

"No," Hope sighed. It was amazing how guilty Ander could make her feel. A crime lord shouldn't be so damn adorable. "I've still brought the contract." She turned the top page on the stack of papers over, revealing a now-familiar list of terms.

It was the contract that would give Hope Jimenez's life to Ander once she died.

The sight of it shocked through her memory, making it tremble around the edges, fraying away.

Hope Jimenez had written her own contract. It hadn't been forced upon her. She hadn't been coerced.

I wrote it myself.

Isobel wanted to escape the memory. She wanted to forget everything that she had just remembered—her complicity in Ander's murders, the fact that she had built her business on the backs of the dead, the way that she had gotten herself involved with his schemes.

Damn it all, Onoskelis had made her *remember*.

And now Isobel could never forget.

Fingers biting into Isobel's wrist brought her focus snapping back to present day. Onoskelis's tiny pale hand formed a crushing vise.

Ander's office vanished in a heartbeat, replaced by the Library of Dis, its many tables, the crystal floor. A new revision to her contract, inked onto parchment made of skin, rested on the desk in front of Isobel. She had no briefcase and wore leather.

The goat demon's gaze was intent. "Did you see?" Onoskelis asked.

Isobel had almost fallen out of her chair. She pushed herself back onto the seat, entire body trembling.

Hope Jimenez had practically pounded the nails into her own coffin.

She still remembered no details about how she came to be acquainted with Ander, but it seemed that they'd been working together since the wedding, at the very least. Certainly before the contract—many years before—and she'd done it willingly.

Isobel couldn't stop shaking. "Yeah," she said. "I saw."

"You believe that I can modify your contract now."

Oh yeah. She believed.

Isobel tried to compose herself, lowering the zipper on her leather jacket to make it easier to breathe. That didn't help. It was still too hot in Hell, the air too close, and now she didn't seem to be sweating well enough to cool her dried flesh.

She'd been deliberately feeding information to Ander to further her career. Her success as a lawyer was largely due to a murderous demon.

The same murderous demon who had ruined her life.

Isobel wasn't certain if she found that more surprising than the fact Hope Jimenez didn't care if her husband stuck his dick in other women, but it was a much more unpleasant realization.

Goddamn it all.

"What would you need in return for the contract revision?" Isobel asked, trying to focus on Onoskelis rather than the nauseating feeling that she'd betrayed herself.

"Fritz Friederling is interesting to me." Onoskelis dipped her pen in an inkwell. The ink that dripped from the tip was, unsurprisingly, crimson in color. "To be precise, his family is interesting to me. They have a history in Hell. Pieces of that history are not adequately catalogued in my records. As librarian, I find this distressing. Friederling has paperwork I'd like to obtain to ensure completeness of my records."

Isobel's brow furrowed. "That's it? You want some of his…paperwork?"

"Accounting ledgers from the years that his grandfather served as Palace Inquisitor. Those records belong in the Library of Dis. Hans Friederling elected to store them elsewhere." It was hard to tell if Onoskelis's upper lip was curling because she disapproved of the missing records or because she was, well, a goat.

The mention of ledgers made Isobel's stomach churn strangely, though she wasn't sure why.

It tickled at her memory. Memories she couldn't yet recall.

They would return soon. Now that the walls had been cracked open, Isobel was fairly certain she was about to begin remembering everything.

She wished she could take it all back.

"If it's this easy to change my contract, then why not release me from it right now?" Isobel asked, rubbing her fingers into her eyes. "You could save my life first, before I do this for you."

"I don't trust you to bring me the ledgers."

"So make another contract for me to sign. Make it a clause that I'll die if I betray you or something."

"Given your history, I wouldn't trust that, either. You obviously have a habit of circumventing contracts."

"Okay," Isobel said slowly. Onoskelis's suspicion was probably warranted, considering that they were having this conversation in the first place. So all Isobel had to do was talk Fritz into giving decades-old accounting ledgers to a librarian. It sounded harmless enough. "But Fritz was just sent to the cells by Judge Abraxas."

Onoskelis snorted. "Judge Abraxas." She scribbled a short note onto a fresh piece of parchment and handed it to Isobel. The letter was a pardon for Fritz. "Retrieve the young Friederling son and bring the ledgers to me." Her eyes glowed in the darkness. "Then I will amend your contract with Ander."

CHAPTER TEN

ISOBEL HEADED DOWN TO the dungeon to retrieve Fritz. Hope Jimenez's memories chased her all the way down.

Too many of them involved Ander.

She was beginning to remember all the errands that she had run for him, even before she died. She'd been doing almost the exact same work for him that she'd done during her months of post-mortem captivity.

In fact, she had spent a lot more time with Ander than her new husband.

Hope had met with him at her law office, at her separate apartment, in public but discreet places. Never in the home she shared with Fritz. Never when Fritz was around.

She had been obviously trying to keep her odd, somewhat filial relationship with the demon a secret from her husband.

But how Ander and Hope had met in the first place eluded her. What they had done to enter that arrangement in the first place was still a conspicuously large blank spot in her memory.

It almost seemed like a deliberate exclusion from Onoskelis's contract revision.

The cells underneath the Palace of Dis were exactly what Isobel expected to find: empty stone boxes that would have fit into any medieval castle's dungeon. Fritz wasn't restrained. He sat in the corner, elbows resting on his knees, waiting patiently to be released.

He stood when she entered, but didn't approach the door.

"You're free to go," Isobel said.

Fritz leaned to the left so he could see behind her. The succubus guard in the hallway was studying the pardon from Onoskelis, debating the signature with a nightmare in hushed tones. They hadn't found any flaw with the paper yet, but they seemed pretty determined to find one. "What did you do, Belle?"

"I went to the Library. That's all."

His expression darkened.

He didn't speak as the guards escorted them out of the dungeons again. The demons seemed content with Onoskelis's paper, and now it had been tucked into the bodice of the succubus's body armor.

They were taken directly to Fritz's quarters again. Someone had gotten the fire going for them —probably one of the Palace's servants.

Isobel ducked into the bathroom to avoid having to speak with Fritz about what she had learned while he was in the cells. She felt so dry. She needed a shower.

But there wasn't even a bathtub. Just a basin

with some sand and a weird scraping device.

She hefted the spade-shaped tool in her hand. It was for taking dry baths, she knew. She could faintly recall using it to scrape the sweat from her body. The powdery sand would absorb the sweat that an ordinary human lost in all the heat.

"How do I know how to take a dry bath?" Isobel asked the spade.

Her memories still weren't quite complete, but she was getting there. And she was starting to think that whatever remained was best left forgotten.

Isobel didn't dare scrape her skin clean when the slightest nick might never heal. She put the spade back in the basin. Stripped off the leather jacket. Started to remove the shirt underneath, and then stopped when she saw the discoloration of the skin on her chest. It was only a small patch, no bigger than her finger, but it looked like the beginnings of rot.

She pulled the enchanted feathers out of her hair and set them on the counter. The glamor fell away. Her face and body shifted from the now-familiar visage of Isobel Stonecrow back into Hope Jimenez.

The face of a ghost stared at her in the mirror. It filled Isobel with disgust to see the woman she used to be. A woman she had tried to leave behind.

A woman who had done a lot of awful things to become successful.

The patchy-pink burn scars appeared quickly, no longer hidden by magic. But those weren't the only flaws that appeared once she shed the glamor. The feathers had also been hiding more rot underneath them.

The flesh was dry and brittle. She still looked better than every other zombie she had ever seen.

Even so, there was no denying that Hell was accelerating her rot.

She tugged her shirt back into place, heart writhing in her chest.

Fritz was waiting for her just outside the bathroom door.

Guilt lurched through her at the sight of his face. He looked so accusatory. "What?" Isobel asked.

"I got out of the cells too quickly. You must have done something."

Isobel brushed past him, dropping the leather jacket on a couch. "The librarian who requested my presence, Onoskelis—she offered me a deal. She released you from the cells so that I could help complete her records."

"Those librarians are fucking obsessed," Fritz said. He planted his hands on his hips and gave her an appraising look. She knew that expression. He was asking her silently what records Isobel could help the librarians complete.

Instead, Isobel asked, "What happened down there with Judge Abraxas? You seemed convinced that he was going to help us once he knew who you were."

It was a good question to distract him. Anger flashed through his eyes. "I don't know what happened," Fritz said. "The House of Abraxas has a long-standing treaty with my family."

"Your family has a treaty with an infernal

household?"

"The House of Belial does." Fritz grimaced. "And my grandfather, Hans Friederling, former Inquisitor—"

"The dead relative who you had me speak with last year," Isobel said.

"Yes. That grandfather. He married a nightmare from the House of Belial. I have no demon blood, obviously, but many of my cousins are half-demon, half-human Gray."

She opened her mouth to speak, but he kept going.

"I know what you're going to ask. Isn't the House of Belial one of the noble Houses of Malebolge? Yes. Did the Friederlings get rich by spilling the blood of mortals in slavery? Yes. Did I have anything to do with those choices? No. I don't have any love for that branch of my family."

Isobel hadn't planned to ask any of that. She didn't know anything about the so-called noble Houses of Hell, including the House of Belial, Malebolge, or...anything else he was talking about.

Except that she did.

That name made her hackles lift—*the House of Belial*. Isobel Stonecrow might not have had any interaction with them, but Hope Jimenez apparently had. And the mere mention of them was enough to infuriate her.

"You're telling me that the Friederlings have profited off of slavery," Isobel said. It wasn't a question because she already knew it to be true.

Fritz gave her a level look, as though he'd expected that reaction. "My family has made some of its billions off of the human slave trade to Hell. And I have nothing to do with it."

"But you've lived a fat life off of the spoils."

"Would it be better if I'd rejected the Friederlings as a teenager and lived in poverty? I'd have been a poor kopis on the streets, passing through halfway houses and homeless shelters like so many other young demon hunters do." Fritz shook his head. "No, I chose to travel, fight demons all over the world, and finance other kopides so that they could do the same. There's a reason so many demon hunters know who I am."

"So it's charity that you've used your family's money for private jets and yachts," Isobel said.

"I'm not a saint. I don't see why I can't enjoy myself while being charitable."

The history of the House of Belial was unfolding in Isobel's skull now, unearthed by Onoskelis's contract revision.

She had already known that Hans Friederling married a nightmare from the House of Belial, even before Fritz told her about him. She also knew that they kept thousands of slaves in Malebolge.

Those mortals were used for labor, harvesting minerals and organics that could only grow in that dimension. Those valuable materials sold for insane amounts of money in the City of Dis. Some of the ores sold well on Earth, too—hence why the family possessed their own portal. How else were they supposed to conduct trade?

The Friederlings had been rich longer than three generations, but it was that merging with the House of Belial and exploitation of human life that had given them the bulk of their wealth.

Isobel was surprised by all the hate she felt thinking about the House of Belial.

It was a hate that had been stewing far longer than she'd known Fritz.

She felt like she was circling around something important, some dark spot in her memory struggling to be restored. But Fritz spoke before she could pin it down.

"This doesn't matter. It's only distracting us." He slammed a fist into the opposite palm. The loud *crack* startled her. She flinched. "Abraxas has to be feigning ignorance. Maybe he's trying to get out of the agreement—I don't know. Damn him, it won't work."

"It *has* worked. He turned us away, and we're out of time." Isobel jerked the neck of her shirt down, exposing her peeling chest. "And unless we get outside help, I'm not going to be around to see why Abraxas is trying to mess with you."

"By outside help, you mean the librarian. What did she want?" He already sounded angry.

"Ledgers," Isobel said. "From your grandfather's time as Inquisitor."

Fritz's eyes rolled to the ceiling. "Of course she wants the ledgers. Everyone wants those goddamn ledgers."

"Why?"

"Because they track the slaves bought and sold by the House of Belial, including slave-specific codes. You can track every mortal who passed through service with the House of Belial. You know what that's worth?"

"Anything," Isobel said automatically.

"For some people, yes. The ledgers would be a way to find any number of missing persons. For a librarian, however, the only interest is completion of the Palace of Dis's records." His eyes narrowed. "You don't know anything about those ledgers, do you?"

Isobel didn't, but Hope did. She felt angry again. Angry and desperate.

Fritz spoke so casually of how important those ledgers could be, as though finding "missing persons"—more like kidnap victims—was just a part of doing business. He *knew* that, and still, he hadn't done anything with those damn ledgers.

"Why?" Isobel asked. "Why haven't you used your family's records to help the enslaved?"

"The ledgers are generations old now. The people most hurt by the purchase of those slaves are dead." Fritz shook his head, jaw clenched and trembling. "People I share blood with died to protect the secrets of the House of Belial. There would be no justice in releasing that information. Not for the slaves who are already gone, and not for the Friederlings still tangled in Malebolge."

She realized that she was pacing back and forth across a Persian rug, probably at risk of tearing holes in it with her boots. She forced herself to stop walking.

"We've always had disparate senses of justice," Isobel said.

Fritz smiled faintly. "Yes, I'm soulless."

"I never should have called you that. It wasn't nice."

His smile grew. Isobel was struggling with anger against the Friederlings, but Fritz was just happy that she was showing signs of being the wife he'd lost years earlier.

I'm such a piece of shit.

Fritz had only benefited from his family's actions, enjoying the fruits of relationships that they had built with demons. Hope had taken the initiative and built relationships with demons all on her own.

What was a little slavery compared to complicity in murder? She was just as bad as the Friederlings.

Isobel leaned against his chest, gripping the lapels of his shirt in both hands. The thudding of his living human heart felt powerfully strong against her cheek, without her own pulse to combat it. "I'm remembering things, Fritz."

"Remembering things? Like what?"

She had to confess to him. He deserved to know what Hope had hidden from him for so many years. "I was ruthless in obtaining clients. I knew they were bad people and I helped them anyway, just because I wanted the prestige."

"I know," Fritz said. "We talked about that a lot."

"You don't know the worst of it," Isobel said. "You don't know how many terrible things I did to get those clients."

"It doesn't matter. I don't care."

He'd probably feel differently if he knew that Ander had been involved…but she couldn't bring herself to say that.

It was a good thing she couldn't cry anymore.

She was still struggling to get the words out when Fritz pulled away from her. He braced his hands against the fireplace, staring into its depths and giving her the time to study his frame outlined by the light of dancing flames.

Isobel had always admired the perfection of his body, the balanced lines that made him look like he was about to fight at any moment. Now Fritz leaned heavily on his intact foot, giving an awkward tilt to his spine that made him seem so much more damaged.

He didn't look any less perfect to her.

"It'll piss my family off if they find out these ledgers landed in the Library of Dis." He gave a dry laugh. "I don't think I care very much."

Fritz grabbed the bucket from beside the fireplace and tossed its contents over the fire. The flames smothered under the sand. He jabbed at the coals with a poker until they were dark, then swept them aside.

There was a handle underneath the place the fire had burned.

He lifted it to reveal a safe. Isobel didn't breathe as he twisted a code into the lock.

"You've had those files in Hell all this time?" she asked.

"The librarians would have known if I removed the documents from the Palace. They know everything." Fritz opened the door of the safe and reached inside. He extracted a stack of papers bound together by a rubber band, and his brow creased. "Wait, where…?" He leafed through the papers. Tossed them aside. Ran his hands along the inside of the safe.

Isobel's heart dropped. "What's wrong?"

Fritz slammed his fist into his knee.

"The ledgers are missing," he said.

CHAPTER ELEVEN

DAYS TICKED PAST ON the clock in Fritz's room.

Isobel watched them winding down. She should have been doing something with her last hours, but she couldn't seem to get off the couch. It felt like all her organs had been replaced with rocks and gravity had tripled.

The things that she still couldn't remember seemed so important now. Those last few black patches in her memory hurt.

Leaving her old life behind had never bothered her too much before, since it was hard to miss things that she hadn't been able to remember. Isobel had only known her old life—her life as Hope Jimenez—by the things that Ander had told her. And he hadn't seemed to know much. He'd certainly never let on to the fact she'd been a lawyer.

All he'd said was that her family had come from what was now known as Iran, but had lived in Manhattan for at least fifty years. He'd also told her that necrocognition was a family skill.

That was about it.

She'd never pressed him for more information because even that degree of familiarity was nauseating, and she hated that Ander knew anything about her at all.

At least...she thought she'd hated Ander.

In fact, her hatred for the infernal crime lord had been unique to Isobel. Hope had liked him quite a lot. And clearly Ander had known Hope very well—much better than he ever let her know.

Which led Isobel back to the one frustrating question that seemed more important than anything else.

How had Hope originally become acquainted with Ander?

Isobel shut her eyes, tipped her head back against the couch, and tried to remember. She forced herself to relive all the memories that made her uncomfortable, especially all the times that she'd spent associating with Ander and hiding it from Fritz.

She still couldn't remember anything with Ander before her wedding.

"Why?" she asked aloud. "What am I missing?"

Whatever she couldn't remember was obviously a huge part of who Hope Jimenez had been.

Isobel massaged her temples with her fingertips. Thinking circles around and around these questions were going to drive her crazy before she died permanently.

The door creaked open. Fritz had returned from the Library, where he'd been planning to confront Onoskelis about the ledgers. "Why are you just sitting there?" Fritz asked, slamming the door behind him.

She rubbed her dry eyes. "Trying to remember. Did you get anything from Onoskelis?"

"All I've gotten is that she felt the ledgers cross the Palace wards at some point. She couldn't tell me if they'd been coming or going." Fritz's hands clenched into fists. "And she won't budge on rewriting your contract without those fucking ledgers. I can't buy her. The librarians don't care about anything but information, and somehow, they've already got everything else they want from my family."

He slammed out of the room, going onto the glassed-in balcony that overlooked the city.

Isobel's whole body ached when she stood to follow him. She practically creaked when she stepped outside.

Fritz's balcony was small and sheltered by glass, preventing the cruel winds from bearing down on them. Looking up, Isobel could see that only a few other rooms had similar balconies. Even in Hell, Fritz had the best of the best.

He glared out at the city, refusing to acknowledge her presence.

"So there's nothing left to do," she said.

"My staff on Earth is searching. They're ripping apart every goddamn Friederling property. If they find anything, they'll be through the portal with the ledgers in no time." But he obviously didn't expect that to work.

No amount of the Friederling fortune could save her now. Not if Judge Abraxas and the librarians weren't playing ball. And not if Isobel couldn't fill those last gaps in her memory.

"Are you going back to Earth?" Fritz asked.

"What's the point?" Isobel leaned on the railing, gazing out at Hell. The dust storm had settled, so she could actually make out the dark city. It was beautiful in a stark way—the way that trees stripped bare by winter were beautiful.

"You'd have a few more days."

"I can't do anything with that," Isobel said. "I'm not going to spend the last of my life afraid." At least, she wasn't going to prolong her life when she knew that all she'd be able to feel was fear. It filled her with a panicky feeling so immense that it was almost painful.

Fritz leaned on the railing beside her. "You could take this as a last chance to talk to Cèsar."

A laugh escaped her even though she didn't really think it was funny. All that time spent dwelling on Hope Jimenez's life, and Cèsar was the last person Isobel had been thinking about. "He'd be such a sad puppy about it."

"Don't have any loose ends you want to tie up with him?"

She shot him a sideways look. "Jealous?"

"Of Cèsar? My employee? My aspis?" Fritz looked like he was considering denying it, but then he shrugged. "Yes."

"Don't be," Isobel said. "I was done with him before we even started."

His hand engulfed hers. His skin was cool compared to the air in Hell. "Sweetheart, I'm not jealous of him because of you."

"I hooked up with him." She tossed it out there, looking for a reaction.

She didn't get one.

"Yeah, I know," Fritz said. "Cèsar's terrible about shielding his emotions."

Apparently, Fritz was very serious about being comfortable in his non-monogamy. It prickled at the back of Isobel's neck. "Then why are you jealous?"

"It's because it all comes so easily to him. The guy is so damn *good*. There's right and wrong in his world, and he's firmly on the right side of it. Must be nice."

"Just because your family is bad doesn't mean you have to be," Isobel said.

"It's inside of me. It's in my blood." Fritz glared out at the city. "Many of the slaves in Dis are here because of the House of Belial and our agreement with the House of Abraxas—for all that's not even worth."

"That bothers you?" Isobel smiled faintly. "Maybe you're not completely soulless."

"Only half," he said.

She turned her hand to twine her fingers with his. "You've never been anything but a hero, Fritz." She meant it. Whatever disgust Hope harbored for the Friederlings and the House of Belial, it didn't apply to Fritz.

He didn't pull away, but he didn't exactly return the gesture, either. He was stiff to the touch. Fritz glared down at her, head tilted so that he studied Isobel down the bridge of his nose. "I'm not a hero. I've never felt so goddamn helpless."

The intensity in his voice would have been surprising, maybe even off-putting, before Onoskelis had released most of Isobel's memories. But now that she could recall their years together, their too-short and tumultuous marriage, it made something blossom among the fear in her chest. A warmth that filled her to the tips of her shriveling fingers.

There were still too many things that she didn't remember, but she didn't doubt that they'd loved each other. Not anymore.

"If your staff finds the ledgers, good," she said, sidling against him, wrapping her arms around his. "We'll know soon. And if not..." She rested her head against his shoulder.

"What do you want to do in the meantime?" Fritz asked. He pulled her against his chest.

She found a smile lurking somewhere inside of herself, somewhere hidden among the darkness. "Take a guess." She tugged the hem of his shirt out of his pants, loosened his belt. "Just...be gentle."

Fritz wasn't gentle.

He wasn't gentle, he wasn't hesitant, and he didn't show any sign of acknowledging that they were facing Isobel's last hours.

He shoved her against the railing on the balcony. He stripped the leather from her body and didn't flinch at the wounds she'd been concealing underneath. She felt small and helpless in his grip.

It had always been like this between Fritz and Hope. He wasn't a particularly imposing man, so when he did show his strength, it was shocking. He handled her as easily as though she were nothing more than a doll. She was at least twenty pounds heavier than she'd been in her lawyer days, and it was still nothing to him.

Hope had always liked that, and so did Isobel. She especially liked that he didn't treat her like death might leave her brittle and fragile—even if it did.

Pressed between the glass of the balcony and Fritz's body, Isobel lost herself in the touch, surrendering to grief and inevitability and the end of everything.

With Fritz, she mourned Hope Jimenez. She mourned Isobel Stonecrow.

And she let it all go.

Isobel and Fritz dozed in bed afterward, neither awake nor asleep. The mahogany monster with its foam mattress and down comforter looked completely out of place against the black stone of Hell, but it was incredibly comfortable.

She drifted on waves of memory with her cheek pressed against Fritz's chest, listening to his beating heart.

The contract's magic was almost completely gone now.

She didn't try to push through against the holes in her memory anymore. There was no point in that. Instead, she reveled in all the little things she did remember—the moments where life had been nothing but Fritz and Hope. Afternoons on white sand beaches. Breathless interludes on her desk at work. Kisses exchanged while Fritz was drenched in the blood of demons.

They'd been so young, so impulsive, and in so much of a hurry. Fritz had been fun. Always fighting, always getting into trouble, always bringing other kopides home to their condo so they could drink on the weekends.

Those were the moments that Isobel remembered.

Not Ander. Not her court cases. None of the terrible people she saved.

Just the love.

Fritz's breathing grew deep. His heartbeat slowed. She lifted her head to see that his eyes were closed.

Isobel slipped out of bed. Fritz didn't stir.

Even though he was asleep, there was still something distinctly guarded about him. He wasn't the fun young kopis she had married, hopping around the world to slay demons in his private jet while his wife held down a job.

It was as though Fritz had taken her responsibilities onto himself after her death. He'd become the businessman. The person who worked a job in an office. That kind of responsibility weighed heavily on him.

Isobel touched a hand to her chest. Her heart wasn't even pretending to beat anymore. Her muscles felt weak, too.

She checked the clock.

Another day had passed, and it was March. Probably spring equinox on Earth.

Her contract was over and they'd almost slept through it. If she'd stayed in bed for just a few minutes, Fritz would have woken up to find her gone.

"Looks like time is up," she whispered.

She wouldn't leave her body somewhere for Fritz to find it.

Her vision blurred as she stepped into the hallway. She wasn't dressed, but it didn't matter—she had to get away from Fritz's quarters.

Isobel climbed the stairs of the tower, legs weakening with every step. The inhabitants of the Palace didn't look at her twice. They lived among succubi and slaves. A naked zombie staggering through the halls was nothing.

A white roar filled her skull that sounded very much like the winds of Dis. She didn't feel afraid, didn't feel angry. She just felt blank.

She found her way out onto a bridge, but the weather didn't touch her. Her skin had gone numb.

The magic of Ander's contract unraveled from her mind.

For a brilliant moment of clarity, Isobel remembered everything.

She wasn't the woman who used to be Hope Jimenez. She *was* Hope Jimenez, and she remembered it all—from her first days in preschool to her graduation from a private high school, all the boys she had dated, her many thousands of lessons in necrocognition from her father.

Everything blended seamlessly with the months she spent as a new woman in Ander's employ, and the years beyond. The life she had created as Isobel Stonecrow. The people she had helped.

She was whole. The veil had lifted.

Then she was sinking, fraying, dropping into nothingness as her body failed completely.

Hell swirled around her. The towers distorted. When she hit her knees on the bridge, there was no pain because her body was already shutting down. Sensations couldn't travel from her limbs to her brain.

"Isobel?"

Someone was speaking to her, but she couldn't turn to see who it was.

She was dying and everything was so quiet.

Neurons sparked. Memories swam through Isobel's skull.

She was getting married to Fritz on a white sand beach. The ceremony was officiated by another kopis, a man who was ordained to perform exorcisms, but equally qualified to join them in matrimony. Hope was happy. She was excited. She wasn't even afraid for Fritz as he fought the surge of demons that followed the ceremony.

But she also felt guilty. Like marrying him was the wrong thing to do, exactly because it made her so happy.

Hope had no right to be that happy.

Another spark of failing neurons.

She was graduating law school. Ander was standing in the back of the room, smirking smugly as she strode across the stage. Knowing that he already had her in his grip.

Their relationship stretched all the way back to her college years.

Fritz was in the front row, too. He didn't know

Ander was there. He was watching the graduation with pride and love and not an ounce of suspicion.

"Can you carry her?"

"Of course I can carry her, you stupid woman."

Another hard jolt of memory. The images were duller and blurrier. Time was slipping away from Isobel.

Hope walked out of the bedroom in Fritz's apartment. She could hear her husband arguing with Lucrezia behind her, and she didn't really care to get involved.

She felt a strange mix of emotions that she didn't expect. It had been easy to agree to Fritz's terms of polyamory when she thought she would never care if he slept with other women.

But Hope did feel strange. She felt…possessive.

That was all wrong, of course. Hope had never planned to possess Fritz. She hadn't meant to stay with him long enough to care if he had affairs with other women.

She only *wanted* him to belong to her.

Fritz had caught up with her outside his condo, cheek still red from where Lucrezia had slapped him. "Are you okay?" he'd asked, touching Hope's arm with such tenderness.

"I'm fine," Hope had replied blandly. "I was just startled."

"I didn't think you'd be visiting, else I would have taken Lucrezia elsewhere." That was his concern—that he'd taken the Italian woman home with him, not that he'd taken her somewhere to fuck at all.

Hope nodded and kissed her husband. She

tried to tell herself that she felt so confused because she had been hoping to snoop through Fritz's condo, not because she had found him engaging in the kinds of extramarital relations that they'd both agreed were fine.

She never quite came to terms with the fact that she was, in fact, jealous of Lucrezia.

Memory darkened.

Isobel felt like she was moving, but she had no sense of which way she traveled.

She was already in Hell. Where could her soul go after that?

Another spark.

Hope was in Fritz's office at their shared condominium, sliding the bookcase shut. The bolts locked with a heavy *click.*

"What are you doing?"

She didn't immediately react to the sound of her husband's voice, even though her pounding heart leaped into her throat and adrenaline washed over her.

He had discovered her in the office seconds after leaving the hidden room.

If she wasn't careful, then everything was going to be lost.

She couldn't let on to the fact that she'd been exploring places that she wasn't meant to be. She shouldn't have even known that the secret room behind his office existed, much less have accessed it so that she could travel to the depths of Hell.

Act natural.

At least she wasn't holding the ledgers at the moment. If she'd spent even a few more seconds studying the ledgers, he would have caught her in the act, and then there would have been no explaining her behavior away.

She returned the book she had been holding to its shelf.

Act natural. He doesn't know. Just act natural.

Hope had a small smile fixed to her lips as she turned. Not enough to look suspicious—just an expression of pleasant surprise, as though she were happy that Fritz had found her in his office. "You're home," she said, wondering if there was any dust left in her hair. She didn't dare run her fingers through it again. "I thought you had an interview."

"I did. It went quicker than I expected." Fritz was wearing a suit, which looked entirely natural on him, even though he complained endlessly about the kinds of events that forced him to dress up. "The Office of Preternatural Affairs wants me to work for them."

She loosened his tie and dropped it on the desk. Her hands somehow weren't shaking. "And?"

He laughed. "Not a goddamn chance. Can you imagine that? Me, behind a desk?"

"Not really, but you'd be safer there."

"There are other benefits, too. The women around the office are hot," Fritz said agreeably. "The woman who interviewed me, this Italian named Lucrezia…" He gave a low whistle.

Hope gave a little laugh and rolled her eyes because it was what she would have normally done —when she wasn't absolutely petrified.

Petrified, and furious.

She'd only taken five minutes to flip through

the ledgers of slaves bought in the sixties. Five minutes. Ander had instructed her not to look—that he'd get copies of those pages for her to study later.

But Hope hadn't been able to resist. She had to know what the Friederlings had done to the members of her family they had abducted from Earth.

Now she knew that they had been bought and never sold.

Hope's grandparents, her aunts and uncles, several cousins—all kidnapped by the House of Belial, and all had died in the mines before being resold.

She tried to surreptitiously glance behind her, making sure that she had completely closed the secret door into the portal room. She couldn't see any sign that she'd been in there. She would have felt better if she could get him out of the room so she could check again.

Fritz dragged her to him, hands tight around her waist.

His kiss was her absolution. The verification that he'd missed the smell of brimstone on her skin. Fritz had no clue that Hope had gone to the Palace of Dis and taken his grandfather's ledgers.

Guilt writhed in her belly as she wrapped her arms around his shoulders to deepen the kiss.

She'd accomplished her mission. She'd finally given Ander the information he wanted. It was years of hard work come to fruition, and now she could relax, celebrate, and start on the divorce paperwork.

Why didn't she feel triumphant?

"There it is," said a voice, deep and masculine, with far more resonance than any other voice Isobel had heard before. He spoke with total authority. He spoke directly into her mind in present day, separate from Hope Jimenez's memories.

There was a man crawling inside her head, combing through her thoughts. There was no doubt that he could see the things that she was seeing.

"You took them. You took the ledgers and brought this down on yourself."

Isobel couldn't respond. The mysterious voice was right—she had taken the ledgers.

She had done more than that. She had taken a lot of things from the Friederlings. Other files, trinkets from the House of Belial, weapons and artifacts. She had passed them all on to Ander for resale.

It was surprising how many people wanted to buy things from the fabled Friederling family.

And it surprised her how much she had wanted to help Ander do it.

"But why?" asked the voice. "Why did you hate the Friederlings?"

Isobel fell deeper into memory.

Hope Jimenez stumbled through the door of her dorm room, Vena draped over her shoulder. Her roommate hadn't woken up since being attacked by the incubus, but Fritz had reassured her that she would be fine. She just needed to sleep off the assault and have a big breakfast in the morning.

Fritz Friederling. She felt weird butterflies

thinking the name—a strange mixture of attraction and revulsion and fear.

Hope wished she hadn't met him.

She dropped Vena into her bed, removing her shoes and pulling the sheets up to her chin. Then she closed the drapes and turned on the light beside her bed.

There was a man sitting in the chair at the foot of Hope's bed.

She froze at the sight of him.

He was a heavyset older man with slitted catlike eyes and a cigarette cradled between two of his fingers.

"I'm Ander." He'd always talked like that back then, introducing himself as though they'd never met. "I understand that you've met someone interesting today. Someone named Friederling."

"Fritz," she said reflexively. She glanced at Vena. The girl didn't move at the sound of their voices.

"Fritz Friederling. Yes." Ander's smile broadened.

She sighed, shook her head. Hope didn't feel up to Ander's game that day. She was feeling tired and conflicted. "You say that like you didn't send me onto that yacht with Vena to meet him in the first place. You're the one who got us the invitations and —"

Ander pushed her hair over her shoulder, patted her upper arm. "We don't know each other. We don't have arrangements. Never forget."

"Nobody's listening," Hope said. "Vena's not even—"

He rested his finger on her lips. "There are always ears." She nodded mutely, agreeing without speaking. He would have his way. Ander always got his way. "What did you think of the youngest Friederling son?"

Her stomach flip-flopped again.

"He seems okay," Hope said. "You didn't tell me that he was going to be there. Warning would have been nice, especially since I only thought I was there to steal these." She tossed a small notebook at him. It was a list of coordinates the *Friederling X* had been visiting. She'd taken it from the bridge while Vena had been partying early in the night.

"Okay? Just okay?" Ander asked, thumbing through the notebook. "I thought you might hit it off a little more than that. You're his type."

She couldn't help but giggle. "I gathered that." God, it was disgusting how much she was swooning over that asshole. The whole Friederling family was evil. She was a traitor just to be thinking about how he'd looked while stripping off his shirt to dive into the ocean.

Ander's expression clouded at her laugh.

"You haven't forgotten why we're doing this, have you?"

"No," Hope said quickly, smoothing her features. "I haven't forgotten." How could she forget that the Friederlings were responsible for the fact that everyone on her father's side of the family was missing—presumably dead?

Ander was the only way she'd ever be able to get answers.

And maybe a little revenge while she was at it.

"Good. In that case, I'd like to talk to you about your long-term prospects with Fritz Friederling."

"How long-term are we talking?" Hope asked. "Rest of the semester?"

Ander chucked her gently on the chin. "How about...until death do you part?"

CHAPTER TWELVE

ISOBEL WOKE UP WITH tears dampening her cheeks.

Tears.

She touched her fingertips to her skin, marveling at the moisture. Her pinky finger throbbed at the contact. She pried her eyes open, spread out her fingers, looked at the nails. The nail that she'd torn off at Vance Hartley's grave was still missing, but now the wound was bleeding fresh blood.

Pain wiggled in at the edges of consciousness, making her aware of all her other injuries. The cut on her hip, the ache in her knees, her burned fingertips.

Pain and blood and tears. The beautiful symptoms of being alive.

"She's awake," Ariane announced, seated at Isobel's bedside. A man loomed in the corner of the room—not Fritz, but Judge Abraxas.

Isobel's heart sank. "What happened?"

"You almost died." Ariane helped Isobel sit up and pushed a small potion bottle into her hands.

"Drink this."

The fluid inside the bottle was a faint shade of gold. Cèsar would have been able to identify it—potions were right up his alley—but Isobel had no idea what it would do. Considering that she'd been unconscious and at Ariane and Abraxas's mercy, she doubted it was deadly.

Isobel drank.

Warmth spread through her limbs. The bleeding at her missing fingernail slowed.

"You should be back to normal after a few days of rest," Ariane said, patting her knee. "How do you feel right now?"

Isobel took quick inventory of her body. It hurt, but not nearly as much as the realization that she still had every one of her memories. "Terrible," she admitted.

"Good. You wouldn't feel terrible if you were dead," Ariane said.

No kidding.

Isobel couldn't bring herself to look at the robed figure in the corner, even though his silence was as conspicuous as though he'd been slamming giant cymbals together. "Did the Judge...?"

"When your contract ended, your mind was completely restored for a few minutes as your body shut down," Ariane said. "At Fritz's urging, the Judge read your memories, determined the location of the ledgers, and Onoskelis signed off on your revised contract. Here."

She exchanged the empty potion bottle for a paper.

It was a copy of a new contract. It was very

much like Isobel's original contract with the end date and memory stipulations removed.

There was nothing on it about Isobel being alive.

"I'm still dead. Aren't I?"

"Considering that you've been suspended in the moments before final death, 'undead' might be the better way of putting it," Ariane said. "You were too far gone to do anything else. Even the librarians aren't capable of necromancy."

But Isobel wasn't going to die permanently, she was healing, and she remembered everything.

Including her betrayal of Fritz.

Isobel buried her face in her hands. Those memories felt far worse than any amount of damage inflicted to her body. Now that she knew Hope Jimenez completely—the woman she had been, the kinds of choices she made—Isobel wished that she didn't.

She had only married Fritz so that she could fuck over his family.

A horrifying thought struck her. If the Judge had pulled those memories from her mind, had he told Fritz what he saw? Did he know that she had been working with Ander the whole time?

She didn't ask.

"Thanks," Isobel told the silent, hooded figure in the corner.

Judge Abraxas exited the room. His cloak whispered on the stone as he moved, and it was the only sound that he made the entire time that he was there.

"He's a good man," Ariane said after the door

swung shut behind him. "Better than most people would give him credit for. And very sympathetic, at times." She sounded affectionate. Isobel wasn't stupid—she knew infatuation when she heard it, and the mortal hostess of the Palace of Dis was definitely infatuated with Abraxas. Even if she was also married to the Inquisitor.

Considering all of Isobel's sins, she was far beyond the ability to judge Ariane for…well, just about anything.

"I guess I owe the both of you," Isobel said.

"I'm only doing my job as hostess. It's my job to take care of all humans in the Palace in whatever capacity they require." Her smile was undeniably beautiful, though a little impish.

"Hell of a job."

"I enjoy it," Ariane said. "It's stimulating."

Isobel picked at the hem of the blanket folded over her lap. "Where's Fritz? Have you seen him?"

"He's gone back to Earth. He indicated that he doesn't plan on returning to the Palace of Dis in the foreseeable future. He did, however, want me to tell you that the portal in his home will remain open until you follow him."

Being able to get back to New York was the last thing that Isobel had been worried about.

"Can I ask where you guys found the ledgers?" Isobel asked.

The door to Fritz's room swung open. "I gave the ledgers to the librarians for cataloging when I heard they were desired."

Lucrezia di Angelis entered. She had shed her white suit for more traditional clothing appropriate to the City of Dis—veils the same shade of crimson as Judge Abraxas's. The blonde hair and red cloth were striking against each other.

Isobel hugged the blankets to her chest, feeling strangely vulnerable in the presence of the vice president. "You did?"

Her mind whirled. If Lucrezia di Angelis had been able to give the ledgers to the librarian, then...

"We wouldn't have gotten them quickly enough if Lucrezia hadn't already been on her way," Ariane said. "You're very lucky, Isobel."

Lucky. That didn't seem like the right word for it.

Lucrezia didn't smile at the praise from Ariane. "I'll take privacy, Mrs. Kavanagh."

"Very well." Ariane patted Isobel's knee. "If you need anything before you leave, I'm reachable by dropping a word with any of the guards."

Isobel couldn't speak well enough to thank her.

Once Ariane was gone, Lucrezia took the chair beside Isobel's bed. She didn't like having the vice president so close. There was no reason to think that Lucrezia would try to stab her or something, but the woman stank of smugness—and danger.

"*You* bought the ledgers from Ander," Isobel said. "You bought something that belonged to Fritz that was being fenced on the infernal black market."

"I returned them once a need became obvious," Lucrezia said. "It's lucky that I was the one who bought them, isn't it?"

"I'm sure you've kept copies."

She inspected her manicure. "I did buy them."

"You're fucking evil. Fritz works for you. He's loyal to the Office of Preternatural Affairs. And you bought things that were stolen from his family!"

Lucrezia's laugh was high and tittering, and Isobel's cheeks heated at the cruel sound of it. "When you consider that you married a man solely to steal from him, calling any involved party more evil than another is terribly naïve."

Isobel's heart knotted.

"So why'd you save me?" she asked. "What do you want in return?"

"For now, I just want to make sure that you know why you're still alive. I wanted you to know that it was only my mercy that saved you." Lucrezia stood, rearranging her veils. "This won't be the last time that you and I have to deal with each other. It will be helpful if you're appropriately grateful next time you hear from me." She checked her watch. "I'll see you on Earth, Hope. Or do you prefer Isobel?"

Isobel didn't manage to think of a response before the woman swept out of the room, leaving her alone in Hell.

CHAPTER THIRTEEN

AFTER HER LONG DAYS in Hell, Isobel was relieved to return to Earth.

Even if her return wasn't very triumphant.

She was still dead, undead, whatever she wanted to call it. Isobel had no idea what that meant yet. Would all of her bodily functions continue as they had during her years under Ander's contract? Would she heal and menstruate and require food again? Or was she no more than an unusually sturdy zombie?

Either way, the deadline had been lifted. She had time to figure it out. And if being undead would create problems, she had time to figure those out, too.

Isobel didn't feel like she'd been saved, but she'd definitely been reborn.

The warm buzz of satisfaction didn't last very long. When she stepped through the portal to Dis, she found the Union on the other side. They were working with Lucrezia di Angelis to break down the equipment in Fritz's office so that everything could be relocated.

Fritz himself watched from the corner, leaning against the wall with his arms folded and a disapproving tilt to his mouth.

"She's through," Lucrezia announced at Isobel's arrival. "Tear the rest down."

Isobel didn't even get a chance to step out of the circle of stone before a handful of black-clad Union soldiers moved in. Each brick was tagged with a number and nestled in padded foam before being locked away.

"What's happening?" Isobel asked.

"We're seizing property that rightfully belongs to the OPA per regulations," Lucrezia said.

Isobel looked to Fritz for a real answer. There wasn't a single window in the room, but he was wearing those stupid reflective sunglasses again, concealing what had to be a scowl. There was no way he'd willingly surrendered Friederling property to the OPA, regulations or not.

Yet there he was, just standing in the corner, totally silent and not fighting back.

Isobel felt a surge of helpless frustration as she watched the soldiers disassemble the portal and carry the locked crates out of the condo.

Her condo. The home that she had shared with Fritz.

"You people need to get out of here," Isobel said.

Lucrezia laughed again. That same smug, tittering laugh she'd used when Isobel accused her of being evil.

Fritz pushed off the wall. He snapped his fingers at Isobel like she was a dog. "Let's go."

"But—"

"Don't worry about leaving the Union unsupervised. They'll lock the door behind them," he said dryly.

She vibrated with frustration as Fritz led her to the hallway outside their condo. He punched the down button. It seemed to take forever for the floor numbers to illuminate as the elevator approached.

Isobel studied him in the cool blue light pouring through the hall window. She could see herself in his sunglasses, hair tousled, feathers bedraggled, dust caked in the creases of her skin. He looked wonderful in comparison. Wonderful and *clean*. It had only taken her a couple hours to follow him from Hell, but he'd had at least a day to compose himself on Earth.

That meant he'd also had a day to think about what Judge Abraxas had told him about Hope Jimenez.

"Fritz..." she began slowly.

"Don't fucking talk," he said.

Her heart sank to the pit of her stomach and then kept going down, down past her knees, her feet, right back to the depths of Hell.

Abraxas had definitely told Fritz what he'd seen in her mind.

"Let me explain," Isobel said.

"There's nothing to explain. You only agreed to marriage so that you could steal from me."

Isobel gazed helplessly at him. If that had been true, it would have been easy to walk away.

But it wasn't true. Even if she hadn't loved him on the day she married, she'd loved him on the day she died.

And now...

"It was wrong," Isobel said.

Fritz's jaw clenched. "You're goddamn right, it was wrong."

The elevator chimed. The doors slid open.

Isobel expected Fritz to let her enter alone, sending her away and terminating their relationship. But he followed her inside.

He waited to continue speaking until the doors shut again.

"I always wondered what kind of luck would have dropped someone like you into my life." Disgust twisted his lips into a furious sneer. "It wasn't luck. Not good luck."

Fritz thought he was lucky for having *her* in his life?

"It wasn't about you," Isobel said. "It was about the House of Belial. My family—"

"Do you want to know the worst part?" he interrupted. "I don't even care that you stole from me. I don't care about the lies. The worst part is realizing that you never loved me as much as I loved you."

Frustration clawed at her heart. "You don't love me as much as you think you do, either," Isobel said. "If you loved me, you wouldn't have wanted to live separate lives. You wouldn't have had girlfriends after we got married. You wouldn't have forced me to represent your spy in court!"

"Has it occurred to you that I wouldn't have asked for any of that if you'd just told me it was a problem?" Fritz asked. "That *maybe* I made those demands because I thought that you agreed with me?"

Her mouth opened and shut with no sound coming out.

"And it was all for Ander. That smarmy, smug..." Fritz slammed his fist into the wall of the elevator. "I didn't even know he was out to get me for that long." His eyes searched her face. "And I never would have thought you hated me so much."

"No, Fritz," Isobel said.

The elevator chimed again, cutting off her attempt to defend herself. They had reached the lobby. Fritz didn't wait for her before marching across the high-ceilinged lobby for the glass doors, outside which his limousine was already waiting.

She was still wearing dusty leather, so they got more than a few weird looks from the other inhabitants of the condo tower on their way out. It wasn't the right place to continue arguing. They didn't need the attention. But she couldn't remain silent, either.

"You're right," she said under her breath, quietly pacing Fritz toward the door. "I hated every last drop of that fucking Friederling blood. My family was sold into slavery for the House of Belial. I grew up hearing stories about how awful they were from my dad." She snagged his sleeve before he could head out the door. "I don't hate you, Fritz. I've never hated you."

He used her grip to pull her to the limousine and practically tossed her inside. "This conversation's done, Isobel." Not Emmeline, not Belle, no affectionate pet names. Just Isobel.

Fritz climbed into the limo, knocked on the window to tell the driver he was ready, and they were off.

"Where are we going?" Isobel asked.

"You're going back to Los Angeles," Fritz said. "I'm going back to work."

"Is that it? We're just…going our separate ways?"

"We've always had our own lives to worry about. It's nothing new."

Isobel gazed helplessly at him. Of course he was angry. Heartbroken. His idea of the woman he had loved for so many years had been completely shattered.

But Isobel was just rediscovering the love she'd had for him. She wasn't ready to let that go. "Come on. Let's just talk through this."

He glared out the window. "Don't use that tone of voice with me."

"Then how should—"

"Don't speak at all," he interrupted.

So she didn't speak, not until they reached a private airport where the Friederling jet was waiting.

The limousine stopped on the tarmac. The driver opened the door. Fritz didn't get out—this flight wasn't for him.

"When can we talk?" Isobel asked. "Will you get a hold of me?"

He clenched his jaw.

"Ma'am," the driver said politely, sweeping a hand toward the jet.

She got out of the limousine. Her last glimpse

of Fritz before she was led away was of a man hiding behind his sunglasses, lurking in the shadows deep inside his limousine, lost inside a very plush and very rich Hell.

It was strange to fly on the Friederling private jet without Fritz's presence. Isobel would have been grateful for the privacy before visiting Dis, but now that Hope's memories had been returned to her, his absence felt like a void gnawing in the pit of her belly.

She missed him so goddamn much.

Isobel took a shower as they flew over the Midwest. Even Fritz's money couldn't lead to a comfortable shower on an airplane, but even the tiny stall and weak showerhead were refreshing now.

It left her muscles feeling loose, her limbs heavy. She stretched out in one of the big leather chairs to nap.

When she slept, she still dreamed of her life as Hope Jimenez, but they were no longer Technicolor replays of her past life. She only glimpsed dull snatches.

She dreamed of the day that Ander had first approached her—the summer after high school, when she'd been looking for more information about her family without finding anything.

His sweet promises of revenge didn't translate well to the dream. She couldn't remember exactly what he'd said, but she remembered how exhilarated she had been that he offered the opportunity to her.

Her dreams drifted onward, taking her to the day that Hope had agreed to spy on Fritz, quickly followed by the day that she realized she did want to marry him and had gone too far wedging herself into his life.

Isobel wished she didn't remember any of that.

The flight attendant woke her up a couple minutes before landing gear touched pavement. It was a guy Isobel didn't recognize. Lucrezia's stewardess spy had already been replaced.

Isobel had stopped crying by the time the jet stopped.

"Can I borrow a phone?" Isobel asked the flight attendant as she pulled her dusty jacket back on. It was uncomfortably hot now, but she didn't have anything else to wear. "I need to have someone pick me up from the airport."

The flight attendant's smile was sympathetic. "I don't think that'll be necessary."

Isobel only saw what he meant once she stepped out onto the tarmac.

Her RV was parked outside.

Someone had taken it to be washed, and it glistened on the airstrip in all its teal glory. Isobel had to resist the urge to squeal when she turned the key in the ignition and the engine gave a healthy grumble in response. The gas gauge told her the tank was full. The shag carpeting smelled like fresh shampoo.

Fritz had arranged to have her RV repaired and detailed while they were in Hell.

Warmth blossomed in her chest, quickly

quashed by the realization that he'd probably done it before Judge Abraxas spilled her secrets.

The RV's condition wasn't a romantic gesture. It was just one more nice thing Fritz had done for her that she didn't deserve.

But then a card on the dashboard caught her eye.

She unfolded the square of white paper. All it said was the name of a beach on the California coast, signed "FF." That was definitely his signature, but it looked like the note had been faxed. Fritz hadn't actually been in her RV to deliver it.

Isobel quickly changed outfits while she considered that card, trying to decide if there was any point in going to that beach.

It wasn't like he was going to be waiting for her there. He wouldn't have even been able to reach her in time.

But where else was she going?

Having donned a comfortable pair of shorts and a tattered Eloquent Blood t-shirt, Isobel got behind the wheel and drove to the beach.

It was a couple hours north of Los Angeles. She'd been in the neighborhood a couple times before; there was an old cemetery nearby where lots of people were eager to talk with their ancestors.

The beach itself was comprised of fine white sand that reminded Isobel of the Bahamas. No wonder Fritz had picked it out.

She parked her RV behind some rocks and walked up and down the beach. Isobel wasn't sure if it was actually as cold as it felt, or if she was still adjusted to the ambient temperature of Hell. It felt like Dis was going to cling to her skin for months, if she ever got rid of it at all.

Aside from a few people walking their dogs, she was alone. The wind beat her hair around her face. She kicked off her sandals and stepped into the surf.

No Fritz.

She knew she probably didn't deserve his forgiveness anyway. Heck, she probably didn't even deserve a chance for him to listen to what she had to say. There was no real defense for what she'd done. Isobel was guilty of every single thing that he was angry about.

The sun sank over the horizon, but Isobel didn't return to her RV. She sank into the sand. Buried her feet among the seaweed. Gazed up at the sky.

And then she heard it—or maybe she felt it. A shift in the ocean.

She sat up to find a white yacht slicing through the waves. It was approaching the beach, angling for a pier just a little further south than where Isobel sat.

Even at that distance, she could read the letters on the side: "Friederling X."

Dinner was waiting for Isobel on board the yacht. She hadn't even realized she was hungry until she saw the food waiting for her, and then she was suddenly ravenous.

That answered one question about her undead

body. She definitely still needed to eat.

Isobel didn't sit down, though. She hung back by the boat's railing, gripping the wet metal in both hands, watching as Fritz Friederling took his seat.

He was wearing a white shirt, white slacks, loafers without socks. Not a tie or cufflink in sight. If not for the shortness of his hair and the few extra years on his face, he might have been the fun young kopis that Hope Jimenez had fallen in love with despite her very best efforts.

"Sit," Fritz said. "Please."

He still didn't exactly sound happy to see her.

Isobel lowered herself into the opposite chair. It felt moist from the spray of the sea. "You must have left pretty quickly to have caught up with me tonight."

"I only stayed in New York long enough to talk with Lucrezia."

An unexpected pang of jealousy stabbed through her. "Oh yeah?"

"She was going to have you arrested when you returned from the City of Dis," Fritz said. "Arrested, and then recruited to the Union. I gave her the Friederling portal to Hell in exchange for your freedom, but I wanted to get some things in writing before you landed in Los Angeles."

Her jaw dropped. "Recruited? Forcefully?" Cèsar had mentioned it as a risk multiple times, but Isobel had always kind of thought he was paranoid.

"That would have been up to you," Fritz said. One of his staff members opened a bottle of wine and poured it in the glasses between them. It was a white—probably matched to the fish another waiter was delivering. "You don't want to work for the Union, do you?"

"How are the benefits?" Isobel asked lightly. Her actual instinct was to scream *no!* and leap off the side of the ship, but joking about it seemed slightly less likely to end with her drowning in the twilit ocean.

"It's slightly better than slavery. I mean, you get paid for it." His use of the word "slavery" made Isobel feel sick. It must have shown on her face because Fritz said, "Sorry. I wasn't thinking."

He didn't sound nearly as hostile as he had in New York that morning.

Hesitantly, she said, "My vendetta wasn't against you, and I wish I'd never gotten you involved."

Fritz took a sip of his wine. "I'd have given you anything, Isobel. Anything you asked for. Any documents, any of the Friederling artifacts, any amount of money."

She prodded the fish with her fork. It was flaky, perfectly cooked, aromatic. "I know."

"You could have told me about Ander at any time. I would have gotten you away from him before things went as far as the contract."

"I know that, too," Isobel said.

"But I can see why you didn't tell me. I've always been incredibly stupid where you're concerned."

She tried not to smile and failed. She ate a bite of the fish. It was just as good as it looked.

"We've both got things to apologize for," Fritz

said. "We've both caused pain. We've both been selfish." He slid his sunglasses down his nose, glaring at her over the frames. "One of us a hell of a lot more than the other."

Ouch. Isobel ducked her head. "I'm stupid. Beyond stupid. Who dedicates her whole life to getting revenge for family she's never even known?" She spun the wine glass between her forefinger and thumb. "I did. And it wasn't even revenge. It was just... God, I don't know, Fritz. Hope just didn't care about the pain it could cause. She only cared what Ander could do for her."

He tossed the sunglasses onto the table. It was too dark to even pretend he needed them now. "Should I call you Hope again?"

What a loaded question. It went so far beyond her name.

Isobel rested back in the chair, arms folded behind her head. The last light of the setting sun bobbed as the ship moved over the waves.

Was she still Hope Jimenez? There was nothing dividing her from the woman she used to be—no magic, no blank spots in her memory, nothing. She could have easily dressed herself in a suit and gone to court the next day. The real difficulty would be getting up to speed on California law, but only because she'd never worked there.

"I've changed too much to become Hope Jimenez again. My needs, my priorities, my goals—they're completely different now. I like being Isobel Stonecrow. I like what I'm making for myself," Isobel said. "I mean...I didn't even like to bake cookies. That's just too strange." She shook her head. "No, I'm Isobel now—not the woman you married."

Fritz rested his hand on hers on the table. His palm was warm and rough. "You were never the woman I thought I married."

"That's probably a good thing," Isobel said. "I think I'm a better person than I used to be."

"I agree."

"You do?"

"Everyone says they're going to change after they ruin a relationship. Most people are lying," Fritz said. "You really did change, though. In fact, you changed into a completely different person. And I'd like to try again."

"Try what? Marriage?" Isobel asked.

His mouth twisted into a wry smile. "Let's start with dinner."

"Dinner. Okay." She could do dinner.

Fritz swirled the wine in his glass, watching her over the rim. The wry smile had turned into an actual smile. "I'd like to know Isobel Stonecrow better. I think I'll like her a lot better than Hope Jimenez."

Warmth blossomed in her chest, nestled alongside her beating, undead heart.

"I think I will, too," Isobel said.

Printed in Great Britain
by Amazon